"OH, VAUGHN, I *KNEW* YOU WOULD COME TO SAVE ME," ROSETA WHISPERED. . . .

"But the bandits have caught you," she continued. "For God's sake, do something."

"Roseta, I reckon I can't do much, at this sitting," replied Vaughn, smiling down at her. "Are you—all right?"

"Yes . . . Oh, I was frightened badly before you happened along. But now—it's terrible. . . . Vaughn, they are taking us to Quinela. He's a monster. My father told me so. . . . If you can't save me you must kill me."

"I shall save you, Roseta," he whispered low. . . .

Books by Zane Grey

Published by POCKET BOOKS

Most Pocket Books are available at special quantity discounts for bulk purchases for sales promotions, premiums or fund raising. Special books or book excerpts can also be created to fit specific needs.

For details write the office of the Vice President of Special Markets, Pocket Books, 1230 Avenue of the Americas, New York, New York 10020.

THE RANGER
AND OTHER STORIES

PUBLISHED BY POCKET BOOKS NEW YORK

POCKET BOOKS, a division of Simon & Schuster, Inc.
1230 Avenue of the Americas, New York, N.Y. 10020

Published by arrangement with Harper & Row Publishers, Inc.
Library of Congress Catalog Card Number: 60-13714

ISBN: 0-671-83596-3

First Pocket Books printing September, 1985

10 9 8 7 6 5 4 3 2 1

POCKET and colophon are registered trademarks
of Simon & Schuster, Inc.

Printed in the U.S.A.

contents

the ranger

~ 1 ~

Periodically of late, especially after some bloody affray or other, Vaughn Medill, ranger of Texas, suffered from spells of depression and longing for a ranch and wife and children. The fact that few rangers ever attained these cherished possessions did not detract from their appeal. At such times the long service to his great state, which owed so much to the rangers, was apt to lose its importance.

Vaughn sat in the shade of the adobe house, on the bank of the slow-eddying, muddy Rio Grande, outside the town of Brownsville. He was alone at this ranger headquarters for the very good reason that his chief, Captain Allerton, and two comrades were laid up in the hospital. Vaughn, with his usual notorious luck, had come out of the Cutter rustling fight without a scratch.

He had needed a few days off, to go alone into the mountains and there get rid of the sickness killing always engendered in him. No wonder he got red in

the face and swore when some admiring tourist asked him how many men he had killed. Vaughn had been long in the service. Like other Texas youths he had enlisted in this famous and unique state constabulary before he was twenty, and he refused to count the years he had served. He had the stature of the born Texan. And the lined, weathered face, the resolute lips, grim except when he smiled, and the narrowed eyes of cool gray, and the tinge of white over his temples did not begin to tell the truth about his age.

Vaughn watched the yellow river that separated his state from Mexico. He had reason to hate that strip of dirty water and the hot mosquito and cactus land beyond. Like as not, this very day or tomorrow he would have to go across and arrest some renegade native or fetch back a stolen calf or shoot it out with Quinola and his band, who were known to be on American soil again. Vaughn shared in common with all Texans a supreme contempt for people who were so unfortunate as to live south of the border. His father had been a soldier in both Texas wars, and Vaughn had inherited his conviction that all Mexicans were his natural enemies. He knew this was not really true. Villa was an old acquaintance, and he had listed among men to whom he owed his life, Martiniano, one of the greatest of the Texas *vaqueros*.

Brooding never got Vaughn anywhere, except into deeper melancholy. This drowsy summer day he got in very deep indeed, so deep that he began to mourn over the several girls he might—at least he believed he might—have married. It all seemed so long ago, when he was on fire with the ranger spirit and would not have sacrificed any girl to the agony of waiting for her ranger to come home—knowing that some day he would never come again. Since then sentimental affairs of the heart had been few and far between; and the very latest, dating to this very hour, concerned

Roseta, daughter of Uvaldo, foreman for the big Glover ranch just down the river.

Uvaldo was a Mexican of quality, claiming descent from the Spanish soldier of that name. He had an American wife, owned many head of stock, and in fact was partner with Glover in several cattle deals. The black-eyed Roseta, his daughter, had been born on the American side of the river, and had shared advantages of school and contact, seldom the lot of most señoritas.

Vaughn ruminated over these few facts as the excuse for his infatuation. For a Texas ranger to fall in love with an ordinary Mexican girl was unthinkable. To be sure, it had happened, but it was something not to think about. Roseta, however, was extraordinary. She was pretty, and slight of stature—so slight that Vaughn felt ludicrous, despite his bliss, while dancing with her. If he had stretched out his long arm and she had walked under it, he would have had to lower his hand considerably to touch her glossy black head. She was roguish and coquettish, yet had the pride of her Spanish forebears. Lastly she was young, rich, the belle of Las Animas, and the despair of cowboy and *vaquero* alike.

When Vaughn had descended to the depths of his brooding he discovered, as he had many times before, that there were but slight grounds for any hopes which he may have had of winning the beautiful Roseta. The sweetness of a haunting dream was all that could be his. Only this time it seemed to hurt more. He should not have let himself in for such a catastrophe. But as he groaned in spirit and bewailed his lonely state, he could not help recalling Roseta's smiles, her favors of dances when scores of admirers were thronging after her, and the way she would single him out on those occasions. *"Un señor grande,"* she had called him, and likewise "handsome gringo," and once, with mys-

tery and fire in her sloe-black eyes, "You Texas ranger—you bloody gunman—killer of Mexicans!"

Flirt Roseta was, of course, and doubly dangerous by reason of her mixed blood, her Spanish lineage, and her American upbringing. Uvaldo had been quoted as saying he would never let his daughter marry across the Rio Grande. Some rich rancher's son would have her hand bestowed upon him; maybe young Glover would be the lucky one. It was madness for Vaughn even to have dreamed of winning her. Yet there still abided that much youth in him.

Sounds of wheels and hoofs interrupted the ranger's reverie. He listened. A buggy had stopped out in front. Vaughn got up and looked round the corner of the house. It was significant that he instinctively stepped out sideways, his right hand low where the heavy gun sheath hung. A ranger never presented his full front to possible bullets; it was a trick of old hands in the service.

Someone was helping a man out of the buggy. Presently Vaughn recognized Colville, a ranger comrade, who came in assisted, limping, and with his arm in a sling.

"How are you, Bill?" asked Vaughn solicitously, as he helped the driver lead Colville into the large white-washed room.

"All right—fine, in fact, only a—little light-headed," panted the other. "Lost a sight of blood."

"You look it. Reckon you'd have done better to stay at the hospital."

"Medill, there ain't half enough rangers to go round," replied Colville. "Cap Allerton is hurt bad—but he'll recover. An' he thought so long as I could wag I'd better come back to headquarters."

"Ahuh. What's up, Bill?" asked the ranger quietly. He really did not need to ask.

"Shore I don't know. Somethin' to do with Quinela,"

replied Colville. "Help me out of my coat. It's hot an' dusty. . . . Fetch me a cold drink."

"Bill, you should have stayed in town if it's ice you want," said Vaughn as he filled a dipper from the water bucket. "Haven't I run this shebang many a time?"

"Medill, you're slated for a run across the Rio—if I don't miss my guess."

"Hell you say! Alone?"

"How else, unless the rest of our outfit rides in from the Brazos. . . . Anyway, don't they call you the 'lone star ranger'? Haw! Haw!"

"Shore you don't have a hunch what's up?" inquired Vaughn again.

"Honest I don't. Allerton had to wait for more information. Then he'll send instructions. But we know Quinela was hangin' round, with some deviltry afoot."

"Bill, that bandit outfit is plumb bold these days," said Vaughn reflectively. "I wonder now."

"We're all guessin'. But Allerton swears Quinela is daid set on revenge. Lopez was some relation, we heah from Mexicans on this side. An' when we busted up Lopez' gang, we riled Quinela. He's laid that to you, Vaughn."

"Nonsense," blurted out Vaughn. "Quinela has another raid on hand, or some other thievery job of his own."

"But didn't you kill Lopez?" asked Colville.

"I shore didn't," declared Vaughn testily. "Reckon I was there when it happened, but Lord! I wasn't the only ranger."

"Wal, you've got the name of it an' that's jist as bad. Not that it makes much difference. You're used to bein' laid for. But I reckon Cap wanted to tip you off."

"Ahuh . . . Say, Bill," continued Vaughn, dropping his head. "I'm shore tired of this ranger game."

"My Gawd, who ain't! But, Vaughn, *you* couldn't lay down on Captain Allerton right now."

"No. But I've a notion to resign when he gets well an' the boys come back from the Brazos."

"An' that'd be all right, Vaughn, although we'd hate to lose you," returned Colville earnestly. "We all know—in fact everybody who has followed the ranger service knows you should have been a captain long ago. But them pig-headed officials at Houston! Vaughn, your gun record—the very name an' skill that make you a great ranger—have operated against you there."

"Reckon so. But I never wanted particularly to be a captain—leastways of late years," replied Vaughn moodily. "I'm just tired of bein' eternally on my guard. Lookin' to be shot at from every corner or bush! Think what an awful thing it was—when I near killed one of my good friends—all because he came suddenlike out of a door, pullin' at his handkerchief!"

"It's the price we pay. Texas could never have been settled at all but for the buffalo hunters first, an' then us rangers. We don't get much credit, Vaughn. But we know someday our service will be appreciated. . . . In your case everythin' is magnified. Suppose you did quit the service? Wouldn't you still stand most the same risk? Wouldn't you need to be on your guard, sleepin' an' wakin'?"

"Wal, I suppose so, for a time. But somehow I'd be relieved."

"Vaughn, the men who are lookin' for you now will always be lookin', until they're daid."

"Shore. But, Bill, that class of men don't live long on the Texas border."

"Hell! Look at Wes Hardin', Kingfisher, Poggin— gunmen that took a long time to kill. An' look at Cortina, at Quinela—an' Villa. . . . Nope, I reckon it's

the obscure relations an' friends of men you've shot that you have most to fear. An' you never know who an' where they are. It's my belief you'd be shore of longer life by stickin' to the rangers."

"Couldn't I get married an' go way off somewhere?" asked Vaughn belligerently.

Colville whistled in surprise, and then laughed. "Ahuh? So that's the lay of the land? A gal!—Wal, if the Texas ranger service is to suffer, let it be for that one cause."

Toward evening a messenger brought a letter from Captain Allerton, with the information that a drove of horses had been driven across the river west of Brownsville, at Rock Ford. They were in charge of Mexicans and presumably had been stolen from some ranch inland. The raid could be laid to Quinela, though there was no proof of it. It bore his brand. Medill's instructions were to take the rangers and recover the horses.

"Reckon Cap thinks the boys have got back from the Brazos or he's had word they're comin'," commented Colville. "Wish I was able to ride. We wouldn't wait."

Vaughn scanned the short letter again and then filed it away among a stack of others.

"Strange business this ranger service," he said ponderingly. "Horses stolen—fetch them back! Cattle raid—recover stock! Drunken cowboy shootin' up the town—arrest him! Bandits looted the San Tone stage—fetch them in! Little Tom, Dick, or Harry lost—find him! Farmer murdered—string up the murderer!"

"Wal, come to think about it, you're right," replied Colville. "But the rangers have been doin' it for thirty or forty years. You cain't help havin' pride in the service, Medill. Half the job's done when these hombres find a ranger's on the trail. That's reputation. But I'm bound to admit the thing is strange an' shore couldn't happen nowhere else but in Texas."

"Reckon I'd better ride up to Rock Ford an' have a look at that trail."

"Wal, I'd wait till mawnin'. Mebbe the boys will come in. An' there's no sense in ridin' it twice."

The following morning after breakfast Vaughn went out to the alfalfa pasture to fetch in his horse. Next to his gun a ranger's horse was his most valuable asset. Indeed a horse often saved a ranger's life when a gun could not. Star was a big-boned chestnut, not handsome except in regard to his size, but for speed and endurance Vaughn had never owned his like. They had been on some hard jaunts together. Vaughn fetched Star into the shed and saddled him.

Presently Vaughn heard Colville shout, and upon hurrying out he saw a horseman ride furiously away from the house. Colville stood in the door waving.

Vaughn soon reached him. "Who was that feller?"

"Glover's man, Uvaldo. You know him."

"Uvaldo!" exclaimed Vaughn, startled. "He shore was in a hurry. What'd he want?"

"Captain Allerton, an' in fact all the rangers in Texas. I told Uvaldo I'd send you down pronto. He wouldn't wait. Shore was mighty excited."

"What's wrong with him?"

"His gal is gone."

"Gone!"

"Shore. He cain't say whether she eloped or was kidnaped. But it's a job for you, old man. Haw! Haw!"

"Yes, it would be—if she eloped," replied Vaughn constrainedly. "An' I reckon not a bit funny, Bill."

"Wal, hop to it," replied Colville, turning to go into the house.

Vaughn mounted his horse and spurred him into the road.

~ 2 ~

VAUGHN'S PERSONAL OPINION, BEFORE HE ARRIVED at Glover's ranch, was that Roseta Uvaldo had eloped, and probably with a cowboy or some *vaquero* with whom her father had forbidden her to associate. In some aspects Roseta resembled the vain daughter of a proud don; in the main, she was American bred and educated. But she had that strain of blood which might well have burned secretly to break the bonds of conventionality. Uvaldo, himself, had been a *vaquero* in his youth. Any Texan could have guessed this seeing Uvaldo ride a horse.

There was much excitement in the Uvaldo household. Vaughn could not get any clue out of the weeping kin folks, except that Roseta had slept in her bed, and had risen early to take her morning horseback ride. All Mexicans were of a highly excitable temperament, and Uvaldo was no exception. Vaughn could not get much out of him. Roseta had not been permitted to ride off the ranch, which was something that surprised Vaughn. She was not allowed to go anywhere unaccompanied. This certainly was a departure from the freedom accorded Texan girls; nevertheless any girl of good sense would give the river a wide berth.

"Did she ride out alone?" asked Vaughn, in his slow

17

Spanish, thinking he could get at Uvaldo better in his own tongue.

"Yes, señor. Pedro saddled her horse. No one else saw her."

"What time this morning?"

"Before sunrise."

Vaughn questioned the lean, dark *vaquero* about what clothes the girl was wearing and how she had looked and acted. The answer was that Roseta had dressed in *vaquero* garb, looked very pretty and full of the devil. Vaughn reflected that this was quite easy to believe. Next he questioned the stable boys and other *vaqueros* about the place. Then he rode out to the Glover ranch house and got hold of some of the cowboys, and lastly young Glover himself. Nothing further was elicited from them, except that this same thing had happened before. Vaughn hurried back to Uvaldo's house.

He had been a ranger for fifteen years and that meant a vast experience in Texas border life. It had become a part of his business to look through people. Not often was Vaughn deceived when he put a query and bent his gaze upon a man. Women, of course, were different. Uvaldo himself was the only one here who roused a doubt in Vaughn's mind. This American-ized Mexican had a terrible fear which he did not realize that he was betraying. Vaughn conceived the impression that Uvaldo had an enemy and he had only to ask him if he knew Quinela to get on the track of something. Uvaldo was probably lying when he professed fear that Roseta had eloped.

"You think she ran off with a cowboy or some young feller from town?" inquired Vaughn.

"No, señor. With a *vaquero* or a peon," came the amazing reply.

Vaughn gave up here, seeing he was losing time.

"Pedro, show me Roseta's horse tracks," he requested.

"Señor, I will give you ten thousand dollars if you bring my daughter back—alive," said Uvaldo.

"Rangers don't accept money for their services," replied Vaughn briefly, further mystified by the Mexican's intimation that Roseta might be in danger of foul play. "I'll fetch her back—one way or another—unless she has eloped. If she's gotten married I can do nothin'."

Pedro showed the ranger the small hoof tracks made by Roseta's horse. He studied them a few moments, and then, motioning those following him to stay back, he led his own horse and walked out of the courtyard, down the lane, through the open gate, and into the field.

Every boy born on the open range of vast Texas had been a horse tracker from the time he could walk. Vaughn was a past master at this cowboy art, long before he joined the rangers, and years of man-hunting had perfected it. He could read a fugitive's mind by the tracks he left in dust or sand.

He rode across Glover's broad acres, through the pecans, to where the ranch bordered on the desert. Roseta had not been bent on an aimless morning ride.

Under a clump of trees someone had waited for her. Here Vaughn dismounted to study tracks. A mettlesome horse had been tethered to one tree. In the dust were imprints of a riding boot, not the kind left by cowboy or *vaquero*. Heel and toe were broad. He found the butt of a cigarette smoked that morning. Roseta's clandestine friend was not a Mexican, much less a peon or *vaquero*. There were signs that he probably had waited there on other mornings.

Vaughn got back on his horse, strengthened in the elopement theory, though not yet wholly convinced.

Maybe Roseta was just having a lark. Maybe she had a lover Uvaldo would have none of. This idea grew as Vaughn saw where the horses had walked close together, so their riders could hold hands. Perhaps more! Vaughn's silly hope oozed out and died. And he swore at his own ridiculous, vain dreams. It was all right for him to be young enough to have an infatuation for Roseta Uvaldo, but to have entertained a dream of winning her was laughable. He laughed, though mirthlessly. And jealous pangs consumed him. What an adorable, fiery creature she was! Some lucky dog from Brownsville had won her. Mingled with Vaughn's romantic feelings was one of relief.

"Reckon I'd better get back to rangerin' instead of moonin'," he thought grimly.

The tracks led in a roundabout way through the mesquite to the river trail. This was two miles or more from the line of the Glover ranch. The trail was broad and lined by trees. It was a lonely and unfrequented place for lovers to ride. Roseta and her companion still were walking their horses. On this beautiful trail, which invited a gallop or at least a canter, only lovemaking could account for the leisurely gait. Also the risk! Whoever Roseta's lover might be, he was either a fool or plain fearless. Vaughn swore lustily as the tracks led on and on, deeper into the timber that bordered the Rio Grande.

Suddenly Vaughn drew up sharply, with an exclamation. Then he slid out of his saddle, to bend over a marked change in the tracks he was trailing. Both horses had reared, to come down hard on forehoofs, and then jump sideways.

"By God! A holdup!" grunted Vaughn in sudden concern.

Sandal tracks in the dust! A native bandit had been hiding behind a thicket in ambush. Vaughn swiftly tracked the horses off the trail, to an open glade on the bank, where hoof tracks of other horses joined them and likewise boot tracks. Vaughn did not need to see that these new marks had been made by Mexican boots.

Roseta had either been led into a trap by the man she had met or they had both been ambushed by three Mexicans. It was a common thing along the border for Mexican marauders to kidnap Mexican girls. The instances of abduction of American girls had been few and far between, though Vaughn remembered several over the years whom he had helped to rescue. They had been pretty sorry creatures, and one was even demented. Roseta being the daughter of the rich Uvaldo, would be held for ransom and therefore she might escape the usual horrible treatment. Vaughn's sincere and honest love for Roseta made him at once annoyed with her heedless act, jealous of the unknown who had kept tryst with her, and fearful of her possible fate.

"Three hours start on me," he muttered, consulting his watch. "Reckon I can come up on them before dark."

The ranger followed the broad, fresh trail that wound down through timber and brush to the river bottom. A border of arrow weed stretched out across a sand bar. All at once he halted stock-still, then moved as if to dismount. But it was not necessary. He could read from the saddle another story in the sand and this one was one of tragedy. A round depression in the sand and one spot of reddish color, obviously blood, on the slender white stalk of arrow weed, a heavy furrow, and then a path as though made by a dragged body through the green to the river—these easily-read signs added a sinister note to the abduction of Roseta Uvaldo. In Vaughn's estimation it cleared Roseta's comrade of all complicity, except that of heedless risk. And the affair began to savor somewhat of Quinela's work. The ranger wondered whether Quinela, the mere mention of whose name had brought a look of terror into Uvaldo's eyes when Vaughn had spoken to him, might not be a greater menace than the Americans believed. If so, then God help Roseta!

Vaughn took time enough to dismount and trail the path through the weeds where the murderers had dragged the body. They had been bold and careless. Vaughn picked up a cigarette case, a glove, and a watch, and he made sure that by the latter he could identify Roseta's companion on this fatal ride. A point of gravel led out to a deep current in the river, to which the body had been consigned. It might be several days and many miles below where the Rio Grande would give up its dead.

The exigencies of the case prevented Vaughn from going back after food and canteen. Many a time had he been caught in the same predicament. He had only his horse, a gun, and a belt full of cartridges. But they were sufficient for the job that lay ahead of him.

Hurrying back to Star he led him along the trail to the point where the Mexicans had gone into the river. The Rio was treacherous with quicksand, but it was always safe to follow Mexicans, provided one could imitate them. Vaughn spurred his horse across the oozy sand, and made deep water just in the nick of time. The swift current, however, was nothing for the powerful Star to breast. Vaughn emerged at precisely the point where the Mexicans had climbed out, but to help Star he threw himself forward, and catching some arrow weeds, hauled himself up the steep bank. Star floundered out and plunged up to solid ground.

The ranger mounted again and took the trail without any concern of being ambushed. Three Mexicans bent on a desperate deal of this sort would not hang back on the trail to wait for pursuers. Once up on the level mesquite land it was plain that they had traveled at a brisk trot. Vaughn loped Star along the well-defined tracks of five horses. At this gait he felt sure that he was covering two miles while they were traveling one. He calculated that they should be about fifteen miles ahead of him, unless rough country had slowed them, and that by early afternoon he ought to be close on their heels. If their trail had worked down the river toward Rock Ford he might have connected these three riders with the marauders mentioned in Captain Allerton's letter. But it led straight south of the Rio Grande and showed that the kidnapers had a definite destination in mind.

Vaughn rode for two hours before he began to climb out of the level river valley. Then he struck rocky hills covered with cactus and separated by dry gorges. There was no difficulty in following the trail, but he had to proceed more slowly. He did not intend that Roseta Uvaldo should be forced to spend a night in the clutches of these desperadoes. Toward noon the sun grew hot and Vaughn began to suffer from thirst. Star was soaked with sweat, but showed no sign of distress.

He came presently to a shady spot where it was evident that the abductors had halted, probably to eat and rest. The remains of a small fire showed in a circle of stones. Vaughn got off to put his hand on the mesquite ashes. They were still hot. This meant something, though not a great deal. Mesquite wood burned slowly and the ashes retained heat for a long while. Vaughn also examined horse tracks so fresh that no particle of dust had yet blown into them. Two hours behind, perhaps a little more or less!

He resumed the pursuit, making good time everywhere, at a swift lope on all possible stretches.

There was a sameness to the brushy growth and barren hills and rocky dry ravines, though the country was growing rougher. He had not been through this section before. He crossed no trails. And he noted that the tracks of the Mexicans gradually were heading from south to west. Sooner or later they were bound to join the well-known Rock Ford trail. Vaughn was concerned about this. Should he push Star to the limit until he knew he was close behind the abductors? It would not do to let them see or hear him. If he could surprise them the thing would be easy. While he revolved these details of the problem in his mind he kept traveling full speed along the trail.

He passed an Indian corn field, and then a hut of adobe and brush. The tracks he was hounding kept straight on, and led off the desert into a road, not, however, the Rock Ford road. Vaughn here urged Star to his best speed, and a half hour later he was turning into a well-defined trail. He did not need to get off to see that no horses but the five he was tracking had passed this point since morning. Moreover, it was plain that they were not many miles ahead.

Vaughn rode on awhile at a full gallop, then turning off the trail, he kept Star to that same ground-eating gait in a long detour. Once he crossed a stream bed, up which there would be water somewhere. Then he met the trail again, finding to his disappointment and chagrin that the tracks indicated that the riders had passed. He had hoped to head off the desperadoes and lie in wait for them here.

Mid-afternoon was on him. He decided not to force the issue at once. There was no ranch or village within half a night's ride of this spot. About sunset the Mexicans would halt to rest and eat. They would build a fire.

Vaughn rode down into a rocky defile where he found a much-needed drink for himself and Star. He did not relish the winding trail ahead. It kept to the gorge. It was shady and cool, but afforded too many places where he might be ambushed. Still, there was no choice; he had to go on. He had no concern for himself that the three hombres would ambush him. But if they fell in with another band of cutthroats! It was Roseta of whom he was thinking.

Vaughn approached a rocky wall. He was inured to danger. And his ranger luck was proverbial. As he turned the corner of the rock wall he found himself facing a line of men with leveled rifles.

"Hands up, gringo ranger!"

~ 3 ~

VAUGHN WAS AS MUCH SURPRISED BY THE COMMAND given in English as by this totally unexpected encounter with a dozen or more Mexicans. He knew the type all too well. These were Quinela's bandits.

Vaughn raised his hands. Why this gang leader was holding him up instead of shooting on sight was beyond Vaughn's ken. The Mexicans began to jabber like a lot of angry monkeys. If ever Vaughn expected death it was at that moment. He had about decided to pull his gun and shoot it out with them, and finish as many a ranger had before him. But a shrill authoritative voice deterred him. Then a swarthy little man, lean-faced, and beady-eyed, stepped out between the threatening rifles and Vaughn. He silenced the shrill chatter of his men.

"It's the gringo ranger, Texas Medill," he shouted in Spanish. "It's the man who killed Lopez. Don't shoot. Quinela will pay much gold for him alive. Quinela will strip off the soles of his feet and drive him with hot irons to walk on the choya."

"But it's the dreaded gun ranger, señor," protested

a one-eyed bandit. "The only safe way is to shoot his cursed heart out here."

"We had our orders to draw this ranger across the river," returned the leader harshly. "Quinela knew his man and the hour. The Uvaldo girl brought him. And here we have him—alive! . . . Garcia, it'd cost your life to shoot this ranger."

"But I warn you, Juan, he is not alone," returned Garcia. "He is but a leader of many rangers. Best kill him quick and hurry on. I have told you already that plenty gringo *vaqueros* are on the trail. We have many horses. We cannot travel fast. Night is coming. Best kill Texas Medill."

"No, Garcia. We obey orders," returned Juan harshly. "We take him alive to Quinela."

Vaughn surveyed the motley group with speculative eyes. He could kill six of them at least, and with Star charging and the poor marksmanship of native bandits, he might break through. Coldly Vaughn weighed the chances. They were a hundred to one that he would not escape. Yet he had taken such chances before. But these men had Roseta, and while there was life there was always some hope. With a tremendous effort of will he forced aside the deadly impulse and applied his wits to the situation.

The swarthy Juan turned to cover Vaughn with a cocked gun. Vaughn read doubt and fear in the beady eyes. He knew Mexicans. If they did not kill him at once there was hope. At a significant motion Vaughn carefully shifted a long leg and stepped face front, hands high, out of the saddle.

Juan addressed him in Spanish.

"No savvy, señor," replied the ranger.

"You speak Spanish?" repeated the questioner in English.

"Very little. I understand some of your Mexican lingo."

"You trailed Manuel alone?"

"Who's Manuel?"

"My *vaquero*. He brought Señorita Uvaldo across the river."

"After murdering her companion. Yes, I trailed him and two other men, I reckon. Five horses. The Uvaldo girl rode one. The fifth horse belonged to her companion."

"Ha! Did Manuel kill?" exclaimed the Mexican, and it was quite certain that this was news to him.

"Yes. You have murder as well as kidnaping to answer for."

The Mexican cursed under his breath.

"Where are your rangers?" he went on.

"They got back from the Brazos last night with news of your raid," said Vaughn glibly. "And this morning they joined the cowboys who were trailing the horses you stole."

Vaughn realized then that somewhere there had been a mix-up in Quinela's plans. The one concerning the kidnaping of Roseta Uvaldo and Vaughn's taking the trail had worked out well. But Juan's dark, corded face, his volley of unintelligible maledictions directed at his men betrayed a hitch somewhere. Again Vaughn felt the urge to draw and fight it out. What crazy fiery-headed fools these tattered marauders were! Juan had lowered his gun to heap abuse on Garcia. That luckless individual turned green of face. Some of the others still held leveled rifles on Vaughn, but they were looking at their leader and his lieutenant. Vaughn saw a fair chance to get away, and his gun hand itched. A heavy-booming Colt—Juan and Garcia dead—a couple of shots at those other outlaws—that would have stampeded them. But Vaughn as yet had caught no glimpse of Roseta. He put the grim, cold impulse behind him.

The harangue went on, ending only when Garcia had been cursed into sullen agreement.

"I'll take them to Quinela," cried Juan shrilly, and began shouting orders.

Vaughn's gun belt was removed. His hands were tied behind his back. He was forced upon one of the Mexicans' horses and his feet were roped to the stirrups. Juan appropriated his gun belt, which he put on with the Mexican's love of vainglory, and then mounted Star. The horse did not like the exchange of riders, and there followed immediate evidence of the cruel iron hand of the outlaw. Vaughn's blood leaped, and he veiled his eyes lest someone see his savage urge to kill. When he raised his head, two of the squat, motley-garbed, and wide-sombreroed Mexicans were riding by, and the second led a horse upon which sat Roseta Uvaldo.

She was bound to the saddle, but her hands were free. She turned her face to Vaughn. With what concern and longing did he gaze at it! Vaughn needed only to see it flash white toward him, to meet the look of gratitude in her dark eyes, to realize that Roseta was still unharmed. She held her small proud head high. Her spirit was unbroken. For the rest, what mattered the dusty disheveled hair, the mud-spattered and dust-covered *vaquero* riding garb she wore? Vaughn flashed her a look that brought the blood to her pale cheeks.

Juan prodded Vaughn in the back. "Ride, gringo." Then he gave Garcia a last harsh command. As Vaughn's horse followed that of Roseta and her two guards into the brook, there rose a clattering, jabbering melee among the Mexicans left behind. It ended in a receding roar of pounding hoofs.

The brook was shallow and ran swiftly over gravel and rocks. Vaughn saw at once that Juan meant to hide his trail. An hour after the cavalcade would have passed a given point here, no obvious trace would show. The swift water would have cleared as well as have filled the hoof tracks with sand.

"Juan, you were wise to desert your gang of horse thieves," said Vaughn coolly. "There's a hard-ridin' outfit on their trail. And some, if not all of them, will be dead before sundown."

"Quien sabe? But it's sure Texas Medill will be walking choya on bare-skinned feet *mañana,"* replied the Mexican bandit chief.

Vaughn pondered. Quinela's rendezvous, then, was not many hours distant. Travel such as this, up a rocky gorge, was necessarily slow. Probably this brook would not afford more than a few miles of going. Then Juan would head out on to the desert and try in other ways to hide his tracks. As far as Vaughn was concerned, whether he hid them or not made no difference. The cowboys and rangers in pursuit were but fabrications of Vaughn's to deceive the Mexicans. He knew how to work on their primitive feelings. But Vaughn poignantly realized the peril of the situation and the brevity of the time left him.

"Juan, you've got my gun," said Vaughn, his keen mind working. "You say I'll be dead in less than twenty-four hours. What's it worth to untie my hands so I can ride in comfort?"

"Señor, if you have money on you it will be mine anyway," replied the Mexican.

"I haven't any money with me. But I've got my checkbook that shows a balance of some thousands of dollars in an El Paso bank," replied Vaughn, and he turned round.

The bandit showed his gleaming white teeth in derision. "What's that to me?"

"Some thousands in gold, Juan. You can get it easily. News of my death will not get across the border very soon. I'll give you a check and a letter, which you can take to El Paso, or send by messenger."

"How much gold, señor?" Juan asked.

"Over three thousand."

"Señor, you would bribe me into a trap. No. Juan loves the glitter and clink of your American gold, but he is no fool."

"Nothing of the sort. I'm trying to buy a little comfort in my last hours. And possibly a little kindness to the señorita there. It's worth a chance. You can send a messenger. What do you care if he shouldn't come back? You don't lose anythin'."

"No gringo can be trusted, much less Texas Medill of the rangers," replied the Mexican.

"Sure. But take a look at my checkbook. You know figures when you see them."

Juan rode abreast of Vaughn, impelled by curiosity. His beady eyes glittered.

"Inside vest pocket," directed Vaughn. "Don't drop the pencil."

The Mexican procured the checkbook and opened it. "Señor, I know your bank," he said, vain of his ability to read, which to judge by his laborious task was limited.

"Ahuh. Well, how much balance have I left?" asked Vaughn.

"Three thousand, four hundred."

"Good. Now, Juan, you may as well get that money. I've nobody to leave it to. I'll buy a little comfort for myself—and kindness to the señorita."

"How much kindness, señor?" asked the Mexican craftily.

"That you keep your men from handlin' her rough—and soon as the ransom is paid send her back safe."

"Señor, the first I have seen to. The second is not mine to grant. Quinela will demand ransom—yes—but never will he send the señorita back."

"But I—thought—"

"Quinela was wronged by Uvaldo."

Vaughn whistled at this astounding revelation. He had divined correctly the fear Uvaldo had revealed.

The situation then for Roseta was vastly more critical. Death would be merciful compared to the fate the half-breed peon Quinela would deal her. Vaughn cudgeled his brains in desperation. Why had he not shot it out with these yellow desperadoes? But rage could not further Roseta's cause.

Meanwhile the horses splashed and clattered over the rocks in single file up the narrowing gorge. The steep walls were giving way to brushy slopes that let the hot sun down. Roseta looked back at Vaughn with appeal and trust—and something more in her dark eyes that tortured him.

Vaughn did not have the courage to meet her gaze, except for that fleeting moment. It was only natural that his spirits should be at a low ebb. Never in his long ranger service had he encountered such a desperate situation. More than once he had faced what seemed inevitable death, where there had seemed to be not the slightest chance to escape. Vaughn was not of a temper to give up completely. He would watch for a break till the very last second. For Roseta, however, he endured agonies. He had looked at the mutilated bodies of more than one girl victim of these bandits.

When at length the gully narrowed to a mere crack in the hill, and the water failed, Juan ordered his guards to climb a steep brush slope. There was no sign of any trail. If this brook, which they had waded to its source, led away from the road to Rock Ford, it would take days before rangers or cowboys could possibly run across it. Juan was a fox.

The slope was not easy to climb. Both Mexicans got off their horses to lead Roseta's. If Vaughn had not been tied on his saddle he would have fallen off. Eventually they reached the top, to enter a thick growth of mesquite and cactus. And before long they broke out into a trail, running, as near as Vaughn could make out, at right angles to the road and river trail.

Probably it did not cross either one. Certainly the Mexicans trotted east along it as if they had little to fear from anyone traveling it.

Presently a peon came in sight astride a mustang, and leading a burro. He got by the two guards, though they crowded him into the brush. But Juan halted him, and got off Star to see what was in the pack on the burro. With an exclamation of great satisfaction he pulled out what appeared to Vaughn to be a jug or demijohn covered with wickerwork. Juan pulled out the stopper and smelled the contents.

"Canyu!" he said, and his white teeth gleamed. He took a drink, then smacked his lips. When the guards, who had stopped to watch, made a move to dismount he cursed them vociferously. Sullenly they slid back into their saddles. Juan stuffed the demijohn into the right saddlebag of Vaughn's saddle. Here the peon protested in a mixed dialect that Vaughn could not translate. But the meaning was obvious. Juan kicked the ragged peon's sandaled foot, and ordered him on, with a significant touch of Vaughn's big gun, which he wore so pompously. The peon lost no time riding off. Juan remounted, and directed the cavalcade to move forward.

Vaughn turned as his horse started, and again he encountered Roseta's dark intent eyes. They seemed telepathic this time, as well as filled with unutterable promise. She had read Vaughn's thought. If there were anything that had dominance in the Mexican's nature it was the cactus liquor, *canyu.* Ordinarily he was volatile, unstable as water, flint one moment and wax the next. But with the burn of *canyu* in his throat he had the substance of mist.

Vaughn felt the lift and pound of his heavy heart. He had prayed for the luck of the ranger, and lo! a peon had ridden up, packing *canyu.*

~ 4 ~

CANYU WAS A DISTILLATION MADE FROM THE MA-
guey cactus, a plant similar to the century plant. The
peon brewed it. But in lieu of the brew, natives often
cut into the heart of a plant and sucked the juice.
Vaughn had once seen a Mexican sprawled in the
middle of a huge maguey, his head buried deep in the
heart of it and his legs hanging limp. Upon examina-
tion he appeared to be drunk, but it developed that he
was dead.

This liquor was potential fire. The lack of it made the
peons surly: the possession of it made them gay. One
drink changed their mental and physical world. Juan
whistled after the first drink: after the second he began
to sing "La Paloma." His two guards cast greedy,
mean looks backward.

Almost at once the fairly brisk pace of travel that
had been maintained slowed perceptibly. Vaughn began to feel more sanguine. He believed that he might
be able to break the thongs that bound his wrists. As
he had prayed for his ranger luck so he now prayed for
anything to delay these Mexicans on the trail.

The leader Juan either wanted the *canyu* for himself
or was too crafty to share it with his two men; probably both. With all three of them, the center of attention
had ceased to be in Uvaldo's girl and the hated gringo
ranger. It lay in that demijohn in Star's saddlebag. If a
devil lurked in this white liquor for them, there was
likewise for the prisoners a watching angel.

The afternoon was not far enough advanced for the sun to begin losing its heat. Shade along the trail was most inviting and welcome, but it was scarce. Huge pipelike masses of organ cactus began to vary the monotonous scenery. Vaughn saw deer, rabbits, road runners, and butcherbirds. The country was uninhabited and this trail an unfrequented one which certainly must branch into one of the several main traveled trails. Vaughn hoped the end of it still lay many miles off.

The way led into a shady rocky glen. As of one accord the horses halted, without, so far as Vaughn could see, any move or word from their riders. This was proof that the two guards in the lead had ceased to ride with the sole idea in mind of keeping to a steady gait. Vaughn drew a deep breath, as if to control his nervous feeling of suspense. No man could foretell the variety of effects of *canyu* on another, but certain it must be that something would happen soon.

Juan had mellowed considerably. A subtle change had occurred in his disposition, though he was still the watchful leader. Vaughn felt that he was now in even more peril from this Mexican than before the advent of the *canyu*. This, however, would not last long. He could only bide his time, watch and think. His luck had begun to take over. He divined it, trusted it with mounting hope.

The two guards turned their horses across the trail, blocking Roseta's horse, while Vaughn's came up alongside. If he could have stretched out his hand he could have touched Roseta. Many a time he had been thrilled and bewildered in her presence, not to say stricken speechless, but he had never felt as he did now. Roseta contrived to touch his bound foot with her stirrup, and the deliberate move made Vaughn tremble. Still he did not yet look directly down at her.

The actions of the three Mexicans were as clear to Vaughn as crystal. If he had seen one fight among Mexicans over *canyu*, he had seen a hundred. First the older of the two guards leisurely got off his horse. His wide straw sombrero hid his face, except for a peaked, yellow chin, scantily covered with black whiskers. His clothes hung in rags, and a cartridge belt was slung loosely over his left shoulder. He had left his rifle in its saddle sheath, and his only weapon was a bone-handled machete stuck in a scabbard attached to his belt.

"Juan, we are thirsty and have no water," he said. And his comrade, sitting sideways in his saddle, nodded in agreement.

"Gonzalez, one drink and no more," returned Juan, and lifted out the demijohn.

With eager cry the man tipped it to his lips. And he gulped steadily until Juan jerked it away. Then the other Mexican tumbled off his horse and eagerly besought Juan for a drink, if only one precious drop. Juan complied, but this time he did not let go of the demijohn.

Vaughn felt a touch—a gentle pressure on his knee. Roseta had laid her gloved hand there. Then he had to avert his gaze from the Mexicans.

"Oh, Vaughn, I *knew* you would come to save me," she whispered. "But they have caught you. . . . For God's sake, do something."

"Roseta, I reckon I can't do much, at this sitting," replied Vaughn, smiling down at her. "Are you—all right?"

"Yes, except I'm tired and my legs ache. I was frightened badly before you happened along. But now—it's terrible. . . . Vaughn, they are taking us to Quinela. He is a monster. My father told me so. . . . If you can't save me you must kill me."

"I shall save you, Roseta," he whispered low, committing himself on the altar of the luck that had never failed him. The glance she gave him then made his blood run throbbing through his veins. And he thanked the fates, since he loved her and had been given this incredible opportunity, that it had fallen to his lot to become a ranger.

Her eyes held his and there was no doubt about the warm pressure of her hand on his knee. But even during this sweet stolen moment, Vaughn had tried to attend to the argument between the three Mexicans. He heard their mingled voices, all high-pitched and angry. In another moment they would be leaping at each others' throats like dogs. Vaughn was endeavoring to think of some encouraging word for Roseta, but the ranger was replaced for the moment by the man who was revealing his heart in a long look into the small pale face, with its red, quivering lips and great dark eyes uplifted, filled with blind faith.

The sound of struggling, the trample of hoofs, a shrill cry of "Santa Maria!" and a sodden blow preceded the startling crash of a gun.

As Vaughn's horse plunged he saw Roseta's mount rear into the brush with its rider screaming, and Star lunged out of a cloud of blue smoke. A moment later Vaughn found himself tearing down the trail. He was helpless, but he squeezed the scared horse with his knees and kept calling, "Whoa there—whoa boy!"

Not for a hundred rods or more did the animal slow up. It relieved Vaughn to hear a clatter of hoofs behind him, and he turned to see Juan tearing after him in pursuit. Presently he turned out into the brush, and getting ahead of Vaughn, turned into the trail again to stop the ranger's horse. Juan proceeded to beat the horse over the head until it almost unseated Vaughn.

"Hold on, man," shouted Vaughn. "It wasn't his fault or mine. Why don't you untie my hands—if you want your nag held in?"

Juan jerked the heaving horse out of the brush and

onto the trail, finally leading him back toward the scene of the shooting. But before they reached it Vaughn saw one of the guards coming with Roseta and a riderless horse. Juan grunted his satisfaction, and let them pass without a word.

Roseta seemed less disturbed and shaken than Vaughn had feared she would be. Her dilated eyes, as she passed, said as plainly as any words could have done that they now had one less enemy to contend with.

The journey was resumed. Vaughn drew a deep breath and endeavored to arrange his thoughts. The sun was still only halfway down toward the western horizon. There were hours of daylight yet! And he had an ally more deadly than bullets, more subtle than any man's wit, sharper than the tooth of a serpent.

Perhaps a quarter of an hour later, Vaughn, turning his head ever so slightly, saw, out of the corner of his eye, Juan take another drink of *canyu*. And it was a good stiff one. Vaughn thrilled as he contained himself. Presently Juan's latest act would be as if it had never been. *Canyu* was an annihilation of the past.

"Juan, I'll fall off this horse pronto," began Vaughn.

"Very good, señor. Fall off," replied Juan amiably.

"But my feet are tied to the stirrups. This horse of yours is skittish. He'll bolt and drag my brains out. If you want to take me alive to Quinela, so that he may have a fiesta while I walk choya, you'd better not let me fall off."

"S. Ranger, if you fall you fall. How can I prevent it?"

"I am damned uncomfortable with my hands tied back this way. I cain't sit straight. I'm cramped. Be a good fellow, Juan, and untie my hands."

"S. Texas Medill, if you are uncomfortable now, what will you be when you tread the fiery cactus on your naked feet?"

"But that will be short. No man lives such torture long, does he, Juan?"

"The choya kills quickly, señor."

"Juan, have you thought about the gold lying in the El Paso bank? Gold that can be yours for the ride. It will be long before my death is reported across the river. You have plenty of time to get to El Paso with my check and a letter. I can write it on a sheet of paper out of my notebook. Surely you have a friend or acquaintance in El Paso or Juarez who can identify you at the bank as Juan—whatever your name is."

"Yes, señor, I have. And my name is Juan Mendoz."

"Have you thought about what you could do with three thousand dollars? Not Mexican pesos, but real gringo gold!"

"I have not thought, señor, because I do not like to give in to dreams."

"Juan, listen. You are a fool. I know I am as good as daid. What have I been a ranger all of these years for? And it's worth this gold to me to be free of this miserable cramp—and to feel that I have tried to buy some little kindness for the señorita there. She is part Mexican, Juan. She has Mexican blood in her, don't forget that. . . . Well, you are not betraying Quinela. And you will be rich. You will have my horse and saddle, if you are wise enough to keep Quinela from seeing them. You will buy silver spurs—with the long Spanish rowels. You will have jingling gold in your pocket. You will buy a *vaquero's* sombrero. And then think of your *chata*—your sweetheart, Juan. . . . Ah, I knew it. You have a *chata*. Think of what you can buy her. A Spanish mantilla, and a golden cross, and silver-buckled shoes for her little feet. Think how she will love you for that! . . . Then, Juan, best of all, you can go far south of the border—buy a hacienda, horses, and cattle, and liver there happily with your *chata*. You will only get killed in Quinela's service—for a few dirty pesos. . . . You will raise mescal on your hacienda, and brew your own *canyu*. . . . All for so little, Juan!"

"Señor not only has gold in a bank but gold on his tongue. . . . It is indeed little you ask and little I risk."

Juan rode abreast of Vaughn and felt in his pockets for the checkbook and pencil, which he had neglected to return. Vaughn made of his face a grateful mask. This Mexican had become approachable, as Vaughn had known *canyu* would make him, but he was not yet under its influence to an extent which justified undue risk. Still, Vaughn decided, if the bandit freed his hands and gave him the slightest chance, he would jerk Juan out of that saddle. Vaughn did not lose sight of the fact that his feet would still be tied. He calculated exactly what he would do in case Juan's craftiness no longer possessed him. As the Mexican stopped his horse and reined in Vaughn's, the girl happened to turn round, as she often did, and she saw them. Vaughn caught a flash of big eyes and a white little face as Roseta vanished round a turn in the trail. Vaughn was glad for two things, that she had seen him stop and that she and her guard would be unable to see what was taking place.

All through these anxious moments of suspense Juan appeared to be studying the checkbook. If he could read English, it surely was only a few words. The thought leaped to Vaughn's mind to write a note to the banker quite different from what he had intended. Most assuredly, if the El Paso banker ever saw that note Vaughn would be dead; and it was quite within the realm of possibility that it might fall into his hands.

"Señor, you may sign me the gold in your El Paso bank," said Juan, at length.

"Fine. You're a sensible man, Juan. But I cain't hold a pencil with my teeth."

The Mexican laughed. He was more amiable. Another hour and another few drinks of *canyu* would make him maudlin, devoid of quick wit or keen sight. A more favorable chance might befall Vaughn, and it might be wiser to wait. Surely on the ride ahead there would come a moment when he could act with lightning and deadly swiftness. But it would take iron will to hold his burning intent within bounds.

Juan kicked the horse Vaughn bestrode and moved him across the trail so that Vaughn's back was turned.

"There, señor," said the Mexican, and his lean dark hand slipped book and pencil into Vaughn's vest pocket.

The cunning beggar, thought Vaughn, in sickening disappointment! He had hoped Juan would free his bonds and then hand over the book. But Vaughn's ranger luck had not caught up with him yet.

He felt the Mexican tugging at the thongs around his wrists. They were tight—a fact to which Vaughn surely could attest. He heard him mutter a curse. Also he heard the short expulsion of breath—almost a pant—that betrayed the influence of the *canyu*.

"Juan, do you blame me for wanting those rawhides off my wrists?" asked Vaughn.

"Señor Medill is strong. It is nothing," returned the Mexican.

Suddenly the painful tension on Vaughn's wrists relaxed. He felt the thongs fall.

"Muchas gracias, señor!" he exclaimed. "Ahhh! . . . That feels good."

Vaughn brought his hands round in front to rub each swollen and discolored wrist. But all the time he was gathering his forces, like a tiger about to leap. Had the critical moment arrived?

"Juan, that was a little job to make a man rich—now wasn't it?" went on Vaughn pleasantly. And leisurely, but with every muscle taut, he turned to face the Mexican.

~ 5 ~

THE BANDIT WAS OUT OF REACH OF VAUGHN'S EAGER hands. He sat back in the saddle with an expression of interest on his swarthy face. The ranger could not be sure, but he would have gambled that Juan did not suspect his deadly intentions. Star was a mettlesome animal, but Vaughn did not like the Mexican's horse, to which he sat bound, and there were several feet between them. If Vaughn had been free to leap he might have, probably would have, done so.

He swallowed his eagerness and began to rub his wrists again. Presently he removed the pencil and book from his pocket. It was not mere pretense that made it something of an effort to write out a check for Juan Mendoz for the three thousand and odd dollars that represented his balance in the El Paso bank.

"There, Juan. May some gringo treat your *chata* someday as you treat Señorita Uvaldo," said Vaughn, handing the check over to the Mexican.

"*Gracias,* señor," replied Juan, his black eyes upon the bit of colored paper. "Uvaldo's daughter then is your *chata?*"

"Yes. And I'll leave a curse upon you if she is mistreated."

"Ranger, I had my orders from Quinela. You would not have asked more."

"What has Quinela against Uvaldo?" asked Vaughn.

"They were *vaqueros* together years ago. But I don't know the reason for Quinela's hate. It is great and just. . . . Now, señor, the letter to your banker."

Vaughn tore a leaf out of his bankbook. On second thought he decided to write the letter in the bankbook, which would serve in itself to identify him. In case this letter ever was presented at the bank in El Paso he wanted it to mean something. Then it occurred to Vaughn to try out the Mexican. So he wrote a few lines.

"Read that, Juan," he said, handing over the book.

The man scanned the lines, which might as well have been written in Greek.

"Texas Medill does not write as well as he shoots," said Juan.

"Let me have the book. I can do better. I forgot something."

Receiving it back Vaughn tore out the page and wrote another.

Dear Mr. Jarvis:

If you ever see these lines you will know that I have been murdered by Quinela. Have the bearer arrested and wire to Captain Allerton, of the Rangers, at Brownsville. At this moment I am a prisoner of Juan Mendoz, lieutenant of Quinela. Miss Roseta Uvaldo is also a prisoner. She will be held for ransom and revenge. The place is in the hills somewhere east and south of Rock Ford trail.

MEDILL

Vaughn reading aloud to the Mexican improvised a letter which identified him, and cunningly made mention of the gold.

"Juan, isn't that better?" he said, as he handed the book back. "You'll do well not to show this to Quinela or anyone else. Go yourself *at once* to El Paso."

As Vaughn had expected the Mexican did not scan the letter. Placing the check in the bankbook he deposited it in an inside pocket of his tattered coat. Then without a word he drove Vaughn's horse forward on the trail, and following close behind soon came up with Roseta and her guard.

The girl looked back. Vaughn contrived, without making it obvious, to show her that his hands were free. A look of radiance crossed her wan face. The exertion and suspense had begun to tell markedly. Her form sagged in the saddle.

Juan appeared bent on making up for lost time, as he drove the horses forward at a trot. But this did not last long. Vaughn, looking at the ground, saw the black shadow of the Mexican as he raised the demijohn to his mouth to drink. What a sinister shadow! It forced Vaughn to think of what now should be his method of procedure. Sooner or later he was going to get his hand on his gun, which stuck out back of Juan's hip and hung down in its holster. That moment, when it came, would see the end of his captor. But Vaughn remembered how the horse he bestrode had bolted at the previous gunshot. He would risk more, shooting from the back of this horse than at the hands of the other Mexican. Vaughn's feet were tied in the stirrups with the rope passing underneath the horse. If he were thrown sideways out of the saddle it would be a perilous and very probably a fatal accident. He decided that at the critical time he would grip the horse with his legs so tightly that he could not be dislodged, and at that moment decide what to do about the other Mexican.

After Juan had a second drink, Vaughn slowly slackened the gait of his horse until Juan's mount came up to his horse's flank. Vaughn was careful to keep to the right of the trail. One glance at the Mexican's eyes sent a gush of hot blood over Vaughn. The effect of the *canyu* had been slow on this tough little man, but at last it was working.

"Juan, I'm powerful thirsty," said Vaughn.

"Señor, we come to water hole bime-by," replied the Mexican thickly.

But won't you spare me a nip of *canyu?*"

"Our mescal drink is bad for gringos."

"I'll risk it, Juan. Just a nip. You're a good fellow and I like you. I'll tell Quinela how you had to fight your men back there, when they wanted to kill me. I'll tell him Garcia provoked you. . . . Juan, you can see I may do you a turn."

Juan came up alongside Vaughn and halted. Vaughn reined his horse head and head with Juan's. The Mexican was sweating; his under lip hung a little; he sat loosely in his saddle. His eyes had lost their beady light and appeared to have filmed over.

Juan waited till the man ahead had turned another twist in the trail with Roseta. Then he lifted the obviously lightened demijohn from the saddlebag and extended it to Vaughn.

"A drop—señor," he said.

Vaughn pretended to drink. The hot stuff was like vitriol on his lips. He returned the jug, making a great show of the effect of the *canyu,* when as a matter of cold fact he was calculating distances. Almost he yielded to the temptation to lean and sweep a long arm forward. But a ranger could not afford to make mistakes. If Juan's horse had been a little closer! Vaughn expelled deeply his bated breath.

"Ah-h! Great stuff, Juan!" he exclaimed, and relaxed again.

They rode on, and Juan either forgot to drop behind or did not think it needful. The trail was wide enough for two horses. Soon Roseta's bright red scarf burned against the gray-green brush again. She was looking back. So was her Mexican escort. And their horses were walking. Juan did not appear to take note of their slower progress. He long had passed the faculty for making minute observations. Presently he would take another swallow of *canyu*.

Vaughn began to talk, to express more gratitude to Juan, to dwell with flowery language on the effect of good drink—of which *canyu* was the sweetest and most potent in the world—of its power to make fatigue as if it were not, to alleviate pain and grief, to render the dreary desert of mesquite and stone a region of color and beauty and melody—even to resign a doomed ranger to his fate.

"Aye, señor—*canyu* is the blessed Virgin's gift to the peon," said Juan, and emphasized this tribute by having another generous drink.

They rode on. Vaughn asked only for another mile or two of lonely trail, free of interruption.

"How far, Juan?" asked Vaughn. "I cannot ride much farther with my feet tied under this horse."

"Till sunset—señor—which will be your last," replied the Mexican.

The sun was still high above the pipes of organ cactus. Two hours and more above the horizon! Juan could still speak intelligibly. It was in his lax figure and his sweating face, especially in the protruding eyeballs, that he betrayed the effect of the contents of the demijohn. After the physical letdown would come the mental slackening. That had already begun, for Juan was no longer alert.

They rode on, and Vaughn made a motion to Roseta that she must not turn to look back. Perhaps she interpreted it to mean more than it did, for she immedi-

ately began to engage her guard in conversation—
something Vaughn had observed she had not done
before. Soon the Mexican dropped back until his horse
was walking beside Roseta's. He was a peon, and a
heavy drink of *canyu* had addled the craft in his wits.
Vaughn saw him bend down and loosen the rope that
bound Roseta's left foot to the stirrup. Juan did not see
this significant action. His gaze was fixed to the trail.
He was singing:

"*Ay, mía querida chata.*"

Roseta's guard took a long look back. Evidently
Juan's posture struck him apprehensively, yet did not
wholly overcome the interest that Roseta had suddenly taken in him. When he gave her a playful pat she
returned it. He caught her hand. Roseta did not pull
very hard to release it, and she gave him another saucy
little slap. He was reaching for her when they passed
out of Vaughn's sight round a turn in the green-
bordered trail.

Vaughn gradually and almost imperceptibly guided
his horse closer to Juan. At that moment a dog could
be heard barking in the distance. It did not make any
difference to Vaughn, except to accentuate what had
always been true—he had no time to lose.

"Juan, the curse of *canyu* is that once you taste it
you must have more—or die," said Vaughn.

"It is—so—señor," replied the Mexican.

"You have plenty left. Will you let me have one
more little drink. . . . My last drink of *canyu*, Juan! . . .
I didn't tell you, but it has been my ruin. My father
was a rich rancher. He disowned me because of my
evil habits. That's how I became a ranger."

"Take it, señor. Your last drink," said Juan.

Vaughn braced every nerve and fiber of his being.
He leaned a little. His left hand went out—leisurely.
But his eyes flashed like cold steel over the unsuspect-

ing Mexican. Then, with the speed of a striking snake, his hand snatched the bone-handled gun from its sheath. Vaughn pulled the trigger. The hammer fell upon an empty chamber.

Juan turned. The gun crashed. *"Dios!"* he screamed in a strangled death cry.

The leaps of the horses were not quicker than Vaughn. He lunged to catch the Mexican—to keep him upright in the saddle. "Hold, Star!" he called sternly. "Hold!"

Star came down. But the other horse plunged and dragged him up the trail. Vaughn had his gun hand fast on the cantle and his other holding Juan upright. But for this grasp the frantic horse would have unseated him.

It was the ranger's job to manage both horses and look out for the other Mexican. He appeared on the trail riding fast, his carbine held high.

Vaughn let go of Juan and got the gun in his right hand. With the other then he grasped the Mexican's coat and held him straight on the saddle. He drooped himself over his pommel, to make it appear he had been the one shot. Meanwhile, he increased his iron leg grip on the horse he straddled. Star had halted and was being dragged.

The other Mexican came at a gallop, yelling. When he got within twenty paces Vaughn straightened up and shot him through the heart. He threw the carbine from him and pitching out of his saddle, went thudding to the ground. His horse bumped hard into the one Vaughn rode, and that was fortunate, for it checked the animal's first mad leap. In the melee that followed Juan fell off Star to be trampled under frantic hoofs. Vaughn hauled with all his might on the bridle. But he could not hold the horse and he feared that he would break the bridle. Bursting through the brush the horse ran wildly. What with his erratic flight and the low branches of mesquite, Vaughn had a hard job sticking on his back. Presently he got the horse under control and back onto the trail.

Some few rods down he saw Roseta, safe in her saddle, her head bowed with her hands covering her face. At sight of her Vaughn snapped out of the cold horror that had enveloped him.

"Roseta, it's all right. We're safe," he called eagerly as he reached her side.

"Oh, Vaughn!" she cried, lifting her convulsed and blanched face. "I knew you'd—kill them. . . . But, my God—how awful!"

"Brace up," he said sharply.

Then he got out his clasp knife and in a few slashes freed his feet from the stirrups. He leaped off the horse. His feet felt numb, as they had felt once when frozen.

Then he cut the ropes which bound Roseta's right foot to her stirrup. She swayed out of the saddle into his arms. Her eyes closed.

"It's no time to faint," he said sternly, carrying her off the trail, to set her on her feet.

"I—I won't," she whispered, her eyes opening, strained and dilated. "But hold me—just a moment."

Vaughn folded her in his arms, and the moment she asked was so sweet and precious that it almost overcame the will of a ranger in a desperate plight.

"Roseta—we're free, but not yet safe," he replied. "We're close to a hacienda—perhaps where Quinela is waiting. . . . Come now. We must get out of here."

Half carrying her, Vaughn hurried through the brush along the trail. The moment she could stand alone he whispered, "Wait here." And he ran onto the trail. He still held his gun. Star stood waiting, his head up. Both other horses had disappeared. Vaughn looked up and down the trail. Star whinnied. Vaughn hurried to bend over Juan. The Mexican lay on his face. Vaughn unbuckled the gun belt Juan had appropriated from him, and put it on. Next he secured his bankbook. Then he sheathed his gun. He grasped the bridle of Star and led him off the trail into the mesquite, back to where Roseta stood. She seemed all right now, only pale. But Vaughn avoided her eyes. The thing to do was to get away and not let sentiment deter him one instant. He mounted Star.

"Come, Roseta," he said. "Up behind me."

He swung her up and settled her in the saddle.

"There. Put your arms round me. Hold tight, for we're going to ride."

When she had complied, he grasped her left arm. At the same moment he heard voices up the trail and the rapid clipclop of hoofs. Roseta heard them, too. Vaughn felt her tremble.

"Don't fear, Roseta. Just you hang on. Here's where Star shines," whispered Vaughn, and guiding the nervous horse into the trail, he let him have a loose rein. Star did not need the shrill cries of the peons to spur him into action.

AS THE FLEEING RANGER SIGHTED THE PEONS, A babel of shrill voices arose. But no shots! In half a dozen jumps Star was going swift as the wind and in a moment a bend of the trail hid him from any possible marksman. Vaughn's concern for the girl behind him gradually eased.

At the end of a long straight stretch he looked back

again. If *vaqueros* were riding in pursuit the situation would be serious. Not even Star could run away from a well-mounted cowboy of the Mexican haciendas. To his intense relief there was not one in sight. Nevertheless, he did not check Star.

"False alarm, Roseta," he said, craning his neck so he could see her face, pressed cheek against his shoulder. He was most marvelously aware of her close presence, but the realization did not impede him or Star in the least. She could ride. She had no stirrups, yet she kept her seat in the saddle.

"Let 'em come," she said, smiling up at him. Her face was pale, but it was not fear that he read in her eyes. It was fight.

Vaughn laughed in sheer surprise. He had not expected that, and it gave him such a thrill as he had never felt in his life before. He let go of Roseta's arm and took her hand where it clung to his coat. And he squeezed it with far more than reassurance. The answering pressure was unmistakable. A singular elation mounted in Vaughn's heart.

It did not, however, quite render him heedless. As Star turned a corner in the trail, Vaughn's keen glance saw that it was completely blocked by the same motley crew of big-sombreroed Mexicans and horses from which he had been separated not so long before that day.

"Hold tight!" he cried warningly to Roseta, as he swerved Star to the left. He drew his gun and fired two quick shots. He did not need to see that they took effect, for a wild cry arose, followed by angry yells.

Star beat the answering rifle shots into the brush. Vaughn heard the sing and twang of the bullets. Crashings through the mesquites behind, added to the gunshots and lent wings to Star. This was a familiar situation to the great horse. Then for Vaughn it became a strenuous job to ride him, and a doubly fearful one, owing to Roseta. She clung like a broom to the speeding horse. Vaughn, after sheathing his gun, had to let go of her, for he needed one hand for the bridle and the other to ward off the whipping brush. Star made no allowance for that precious part of his burden at Vaughn's back, and he crashed through every opening between mesquites that presented itself. Vaughn dodged and ducked, but he never bent low enough for a branch to strike Roseta.

At every open spot in the mesquite, or long aisle between the cacti, Vaughn looked back to see if any of his pursuers were in sight. There was none, but he heard a horse pounding not far behind and to the right. And again he heard another on the other side. Holding the reins in his teeth Vaughn reloaded the gun. To be ready for snap shots he took advantage of every opportunity to peer on each side and behind him. But Star appeared gradually to be outdistancing his pursuers. The desert grew more open with a level gravel floor. Here Vaughn urged Star to his limit.

It became a dead run then, with the horse choosing the way. Vaughn risked less now from the stinging mesquite branches. The green wall flashed by on each side. He did not look back. While Star was at his best Vaughn wanted to get far enough ahead to slow down and save the horse. In an hour it would be dusk—too late for even a *vaquero* to track him until daylight had come again.

Roseta stuck like a leech, and the ranger had to add admiration to his other feelings toward her. Vaughn put his hand back to grasp and steady her. It did not take much time for the powerful strides of the horse to cover the miles. Finally Vaughn pulled him into a gallop and then into a lope.

"*Chata,* are you all right?" he asked, afraid to look back, after using that romantic epithet.

"Yes. But I can't—hold on—much longer," she panted. "If they catch us—shoot me first."

"Roseta, they will never catch us now," he promised.

"But—if they do—promise me," she entreated.

"I promise they'll never take us alive. But, child, keep up your nerve. It'll be sunset soon—and then dark. We'll get away sure."

"Vaughn, I'm not frightened. Only—I hate those people—and I mustn't fall—into their hands again. It means worse—than death."

"Hush! Save your breath," he replied, and wrapping a long arm backward round her slender waist he held her tight. "Come, Star, cut loose," he called, and dug the horse's flank with a heel.

Again they raced across the desert, this time in less of a straight line, though still to the north. The dry wind made tears dim Vaughn's eyes. He kept to open lanes and patches to avoid being struck by branches. And he spared Star only when he heard the animal's heaves of distress. Star was not easy to break from that headlong flight, but at length Vaughn got him down to a nervous walk. Then he let Roseta slip back into the saddle. His arm was numb from the long strain.

"We're—far ahead," he panted. "They'll trail—us till dark." He peered back across the yellow and green desert, slowly darkening in the sunset. "But we're safe—thank Gawd."

"Oh, what a glorious ride!" cried Roseta between breaths. "I felt that—even with death so close. . . . Vaughn, I'm such a little—fool. I longed—for excitement. Oh, I'm well punished. . . . But for you—"

"Save your breath, honey. We may need to run again. After dark you can rest and talk."

She said no more. Vaughn walked Star until the

horse had regained his wind, and then urged him into a lope, which was his easiest gait.

The sun sank red in the west; twilight stole under the mesquite and the *pale verde;* dusk came upon its heels; the heat tempered and there was a slight breeze. When the stars came out Vaughn took his direction from them, and pushed on for several miles. A crescent moon, silver and slender, came up over the desert.

Young as it was, it helped brighten the open patches and the swales. Vaughn halted the tireless horse in a spot where a patch of grass caught the moonlight.

"We'll rest a bit," he said, sliding off, but still holding on to the girl. "Come."

She just fell off into his arms, and when he let her feet down she leaned against him. "Oh, Vaughn!" He held her a moment, sorely tempted. But he might take her weakness for something else.

"Can you stand? . . . You'd better walk around a little," he said.

"My legs are dead."

"I want to go back a few steps and listen. The night is still. I could hear horses at a long distance."

"Don't go far," she entreated him.

Vaughn went back where he could not hear the heaving, blowing horse, and turned his keen ear to the breeze. It blew gently from the south. Only a very faint rustle of leaves disturbed the desert silence. He held his breath and listened intensely. There was no sound! Even if he were trailed by a hound of a *vaquero* he was still far ahead. All he required now was a little rest for Star. He could carry the girl. On the way back across the open he tried to find the tracks Star had left. A man could trail them, but only on foot. Vaughn's last stern doubt took wing and vanished. He returned to Roseta.

"No sound. It is as I expected. Night has saved us," he said.

"Night and *canyu*. Oh, I watched you, ranger man."

"You helped, Roseta. That Mexican who led your horse was suspicious. But when you looked at him— he forgot. Small wonder . . . Have you stretched your legs?"

"I tried. I walked some, then flopped here. . . . Oh, I want to rest and sleep."

"I don't know about your sleeping, but you can rest riding," he replied, and removing his coat folded it around the pommel of his saddle, making a flat seat there. Star was munching the grass. He was already fit for another race. Vaughn saw to the cinches, and then mounted again, and folded the sleeves of his coat up over the pommel. "Give me your hand. . . . Put your foot in the stirrup. Now." He caught her and lifted her in front of him, and settling her comfortably upon the improvised seat, he put his left arm around her. Many a wounded comrade had he packed this way. "How is—that?" he asked unsteadily.

"It's very nice," she replied, her dark eyes looking inscrutable in the moonlight. And she relaxed against his arm and shoulder.

Vaughn headed Star north at a brisk walk. He could not be more than six hours from the river in a straight line. Canyons and rough going might deter him. But even so he could make the Rio Grande before dawn. Then and then only did he surrender to the astonishing presence of Roseta Uvaldo, to the indubitable fact that he had saved her, and then to thoughts wild and whirling of the future. He gazed down upon the oval face so blanched in the moonlight, into the staring black eyes whose look might mean anything.

"Vaughn, was it that guard or you—who called me *chata?*" she asked, dreamily.

"It was I—who dared," he replied huskily.

"Dared! Then you were not just carried away—for the moment?"

"No, Roseta. . . . I confess I was as—as bold as that poor devil."

"Vaughn, do you know what *chata* means?" she asked gravely.

"It is the name a *vaquero* has for his sweetheart."

"You mean it, señor?" she asked, imperiously.

"Lord help me, Roseta, I did, and I do. . . . I've loved you long."

"But you never told me!" she exclaimed, with wonder and reproach. "Why?"

"What hope had I? A poor ranger. Texas Medill! . . . Didn't you call me 'killer of Mexicans'?"

"I reckon I did. And it is because you *are* that I'm alive to thank God for it. . . . Vaughn, I always liked you, respected you as one of Texas' great rangers—feared you, too. I never knew my real feelings. . . . But I—I love you *now*."

The night wore on, with the moon going down, weird and coldly bright against the dark vaulted sky. Roseta lay asleep in Vaughn's arm. For hours he had gazed, after peering ahead and behind, always vigilant, always the ranger, on that wan face against his shoulder. The silent moonlit night, the lonely ride, the ghastly forms of cactus were real, though Vaughn never trusted his senses there. This was only the dream of the ranger. Yet the sweet fire of Roseta's kisses still lingered on his lips.

At length he changed her again from his right arm back to his left. And she awakened, but not fully. In all the years of his ranger service, so much of which he lived over on this ride, there had been nothing to compare with this. For his reward had been exalting. His longings had received magnificent fulfillment. His duty had not been to selfish and unappreciative officials, but to a great state—to its people—to the native soil upon which he had been born. And that hard duty, so poorly recompensed, so bloody and harrowing at times, had by some enchantment bestowed upon one ranger at least a beautiful girl of the border, frankly and honestly Texan, yet part Spanish, retaining something of the fire and spirit of the Dons who had once called Texas their domain.

In the gray of dawn, Vaughn lifted Roseta down from the weary horse upon the south bank of the Rio Grande.

"We are here, Roseta," he said gladly. "It will soon be light enough to ford the river. Star came out just below Brownsville. There's a horse, Roseta! He shall never be risked again. . . . In an hour you will be home."

"Home? Oh, how good! . . . But what shall I say, Vaughn?" she replied, evidently awakening to the facts of her predicament.

"Dear, who was the feller you ran—rode off with yesterday mawnin'?" he asked.

"Didn't I tell you?" And she laughed. "It happened to be Elmer Wade—*that* morning. . . . Oh, he was the unlucky one. The bandits beat him with quirts, dragged him off his horse. Then they led me away and I didn't see him again."

Vaughn had no desire to acquaint her then with the tragic fate that had overtaken that young man.

"You were not—elopin'?"

"Vaughn! It was only fun."

"Uvaldo thinks you eloped. He was wild. He raved."

"The devil he did!" exclaimed Roseta rebelliously. "Vaughn, what did *you* think?"

"Dearest, I—I was only concerned with trackin'

you," he replied, and even in the gray gloom of the dawn those big dark eyes made his heart beat faster.

"Vaughn, I have peon blood in me," she said, and she might have been a princess for the pride with which she confessed it. "My father always feared I'd run true to the Indian. Are you afraid of your *chata?*"

"No, darlin'."

"Then I shall punish Uvaldo. . . . I shall elope."

"Roseta!" cried Vaughn.

"Listen." She put her arms around his neck, and that was a long reach for her. "Will you give up the ranger service? I—I couldn't bear it, Vaughn. You have earned release from the service all Texans are so proud of."

"Yes, Roseta. I'll resign," he replied with boyish, eager shyness. "I've some money—enough to buy a ranch."

"Far from the border?" she entreated.

"Yes, far. I know just the valley—way north, under the *Llano Estacado*. . . . But, Roseta, I shall have to pack a gun—till I'm forgotten."

"Very well, I'll not be afraid—way north," she replied. Then her sweet gravity changed to mischief. "We will punish Father. Vaughn, we'll elope right now! We'll cross the river—get married—and drive out home to breakfast. . . . How Dad will rave! But he would have me elope, though he'd never guess I'd choose a ranger."

Vaughn swung her up on Star, and leaned close to peer up at her, to find one more assurance of the joy that had befallen him. He was not conscious of asking, when she bent her head to bestow kisses upon his lips.

canyon walls

~~ 1 ~~

"WAL, HEAH'S ANOTHER FORKIN' OF THE TRAIL," said Monty, as he sat cross-legged on his saddle and surveyed the prospect. "Thet Mormon shepherd gave me a good steer. But doggone it, I hate to impose on anyone, even Mormons."

The scene was Utah, north of the great canyon, with the wild ruggedness and magnificence of that region visible on all sides. Monty could see clear to the Pink Cliffs that walled the ranches and ranges northward from this country of breaks. He had come up out of the abyss, across the desert between Mt. Trumbull and Hurricane Ledge, and he did not look back. Kanab must be thirty or forty miles, as a crow flies, across this valley dotted with sage. But Monty did not know Utah, or anything of this north rim country.

He rolled his last cigarette. He was hungry and worn out, and his horse was the same. Should he ride on to Kanab and throw in with one of the big cattle companies north of there, or should he take to one of the lonely canyons and hunt for a homesteader in need of a rider? The choice seemed hard to make, because Monty was tired of gun fights, of two-bit rustling, of gambling, and the other dubious means by which he had managed to live in Arizona. Not that Monty entertained any idea that he had ever reverted to real dishonesty! He had the free-range cowboy's elasticity of judgment. He could find excuses even for his latest escapade. But one or two more stunts like the one at Longhill would be bound to make him an outlaw. He reflected that if he were blamed for the Green Valley affair, also, which was not improbable, he might find himself already an outlaw, whether he personally agreed or not.

If he rode on to the north ranches, sooner or later someone from Arizona would come along; on the other hand, if he went down into the breaks of the canyon he might find a job and a hiding place where he would be safe until the whole thing blew over and was forgotten. Then he would take good care not to fall into another mess. Bad company and too free use of the bottle had brought Monty to this pass, which he really believed was completely undeserved.

Monty dropped his leg back and slipped his boot into the stirrup. He took the trail to the left and felt relief that the choice was made. It meant that he was avoiding towns and ranches, outfits of curious cowboys, and others who might have undue interest in wandering riders.

In about an hour, as the shepherd had directed, the trail showed up. It appeared to run along the rim of a canyon. Monty gazed down with approving eyes. The walls were steep and very deep, so deep that he could scarcely see the green squares of alfalfa, the orchards and pastures, the groves of cottonwoods, and a gray log cabin down below. He saw cattle and horses toward the upper end. At length the trail started down, and for a while thereafter Monty lost his perspective, and dismounting, he walked down the zigzag path leading his horse.

He saw, at length, that the canyon was boxed in by a wild notch of cliff and thicket and jumbled wall, from under which a fine stream of water flowed. There were still many acres that might have been under cultivation. Monty followed the trail along the brook, crossed it above where the floor of the canyon widened and the alfalfa fields lay richly green, and so on down a couple of miles to the cottonwoods. When he emerged from the fringe of trees, he was close to the cabin, and he could see where the canyon opened wide, with sheer red-gold walls, right out on the desert. It was sure enough a lonely retreat, far off the road, out of the grass country, a niche in the endless colored canyon walls.

The cottonwoods were shedding their fuzzy seeds that covered the ground like snow. An irrigation ditch ran musically through the yard. Chickens, turkeys, calves had the run of the place. The dry odor of the canyon here appeared to take on the fragrance of wood smoke and fresh baked bread.

Monty limped on, up to the cabin porch, which was spacious and comfortable, where no doubt the people who lived here spent many hours during fine weather. He saw a girl through the open door. She wore gray linsey, ragged and patched. His second glance made note of her superb build, her bare feet, her brown arms, and eyes that did not need half their piercing quality to see through Monty.

"Howdy, miss," hazarded Monty, though this was Mormon country.

"Howdy, stranger," she replied, very pleasantly, so that Monty decided to forget that he was looking for a fictitious dog.

"Could a thirsty rider get a drink around heah?"

"There's the brook. Best water in Utah."

"An' how about a bite to eat?"

"Tie up your horse and go around to the back porch."

Monty did as he was bidden, not without a few more

glances at the girl, who he observed made no movement. But as he turned the corner of the house he heard her call, "Ma, there's a tramp gentile cowpoke coming back for a bite to eat."

When Monty reached the rear porch, another huge enclosure under the cottonwoods, he was quite prepared to encounter a large woman, of commanding presence, but of most genial and kindly face.

"Good afternoon, ma'am," began Monty, lifting his sombrero. "Shore you're the mother to thet gurl out in front—you look alike an' you're both orful handsome—but I won't be took fer no tramp gentile cowpuncher."

The woman greeted him with a pleasant laugh. "So, young man, you're a Mormon?"

"No, I ain't no Mormon, either. But particular, I ain't no tramp cowpoke," replied Monty with spirit, and just then the young person who had roused it appeared in the back doorway, with a slow, curious smile on her face. "I'm just lost an' tuckered out an' hungry."

For reply she motioned to a pan and bucket of water on a nearby bench, and a clean towel hanging on the rail. Monty was quick to take the hint, but performed his ablutions most deliberately. When he was ready at last, his face shining and refreshed, the woman was setting a table for him, and she bade him take a seat.

"Ma'am, I only asked fer a bite," he said.

"It's no matter. We've plenty."

And presently Monty sat down to a meal that surpassed any feast he had ever attended. It was his first experience at a Mormon table, the fame of which was known on every range. He had to admit that distance and exaggeration had not lent enchantment here. Without shame he ate until he could hold no more, and when he arose he made the Mormon mother a gallant bow.

"Lady, I never had sech a good dinner in all my life," he said fervently. "An' I reckon it won't make no difference if I never get another. Jest rememberin' this one will be enough."

"Blarney. You gentiles shore have the gift of gab. Sit down and rest a little."

Monty was glad to comply, and leisurely disposed his long, lithe, dusty self in a comfortable chair. He laid his sombrero on the floor, and hitched his gun around, and looked up, genially aware that he was being taken in by two pairs of eyes.

"I met a shepherd lad on top an' he directed me to Andrew Boller's ranch. Is this heah the place?"

"No. Boller's is a few miles further on. It's the first big ranch over the Arizona line."

"Shore I missed it. Wal, it was lucky for me. Are you near the Arizona line heah?"

"We're just over it."

"Oh, I see. Not in Utah atall," said Monty thoughtfully. "Any men about?"

"No. I'm the Widow Keetch, and this is my daughter Rebecca."

Monty guardedly acknowledged the introduction, without mentioning his own name, an omission the shrewd, kindly woman evidently noted. Monty was quick to feel that she must have had vast experience with menfolk. The girl, however, wore an indifferent, almost scornful air.

"This heah's a good-sized ranch. Must be a hundred acres jist in alfalfa," continued Monty. "You don't mean to tell me you two womenfolks run this ranch alone?"

"We do, mostly. We hire the plowing, and we have firewood hauled. And we always have a boy around. But year in and out we do most of the work ourselves."

"Wal, I'll be dogged!" exclaimed Monty. "Excuse

me—but it shore is somethin' to heah. The ranch ain't so bad run down at thet. If you'll allow me to say so, Mrs. Keetch, it could be made a first-rate ranch. There's acres of uncleared land."

"My husband used to think so," replied the widow sighing. "But since he's gone we have just about managed to live."

"Wal, wal! Now I wonder what made me ride down the wrong trail. . . . Mrs. Keetch, I reckon you could use a fine, young, sober, honest, hard-workin' cow-hand who knows all there is about ranchin'."

Monty addressed the woman in cool easy speech, quite deferentially, and then he shifted his gaze to the dubious face of the daughter. He was discovering that it had a compelling charm. She laughed outright, as if to say that she knew what a liar he was! That not only discomfited Monty, but roused his ire. The sassy Mormon filly!

"I guess I could use such a young man," returned Mrs. Keetch shortly, with her penetrating eyes on him.

"Wal, you're lookin' at him right now," said Monty fervently. "An' he's seein' nothin' less than the hand of Providence heah."

The woman stood up decisively. "Fetch your horse around," she said, and walked off the porch to wait for him. Monty made haste, his mind in a whirl. What was going to happen now? That girl! He ought to ride right on out of this canyon; and he was making up his mind to do it when he came back round the house to see that the girl had come to the porch rail. Her great eyes were looking at his horse. The stranger did not need to be told that she had a passion for horses. It would help some. But she did not appear to see Monty at all.

"You've a fine horse," said Mrs. Keetch. "Poor fellow! He's lame and tuckered out. We'll turn him loose in the pasture."

Monty followed her down a shady lane of cotton-woods, where the water ran noisily on each side, and he trembled inwardly at the content of the woman's last words. He had heard of the Good Samaritan ways of the Mormons. And in that short walk Monty did a deal of thinking. They reached an old barn beyond which lay a green pasture with an orchard running down one side. Peach trees were in bloom, lending a delicate border of pink to the fresh spring foliage.

"What wages would you work for?" asked the Mormon woman earnestly.

"Wal, come to think of thet, for my board an' keep. . . . Anyhow till we get the ranch payin'," replied Monty.

"Very well, stranger, that's a fair deal. Unsaddle your horse and stay," said the woman.

"Wait a minnit, ma'am," drawled Monty. "I got to substitute somethin' fer thet recommend I gave you. . . . Shore I know cattle an' ranchin' backward. But I reckon I should have said I'm a no-good, gun-throwin' cowpuncher who got run out of Arizona."

"What for?" demanded Mrs. Keetch.

"Wal, a lot of it was bad company an' bad licker. But at thet I wasn't so drunk I didn't know I was rustlin' cattle."

"Why do you tell me this?" she demanded.

"Wal, it is kinda funny. But I jist couldn't fool a kind woman like you. Thet's all."

"You don't look like a hard-drinking man."

"Aw, I'm not. I never said so, ma'am. Fact is, I ain't much of a drinkin' cowboy, atall."

"You came across the canyon?" she asked.

"Shore, an' by golly, thet was the orfullest ride, an' slide, an' swim, an' climb I ever had. I really deserve a heaven like this, ma'am."

"Any danger of a sheriff trailing you?"

"Wal, I've thought about thet. I reckon one chance in a thousand."

"He'd be the first one I ever heard of from across the canyon, at any rate. This is a lonesome, out-of-the-way place—and if you stayed away from the Mormon ranches and towns—"

"See heah, ma'am," interrupted Monty sharply. "You shore ain't goin' to take me on?"

"I am. You might be a welcome change. Lord knows I've hired every kind of a man. But not one of them ever lasted. You might."

"What was wrong with them hombres?"

"I don't know. I never saw much wrong except they neglected their work to moon around after Rebecca. But she could not get along with them, and she always drove them away."

"Aw, I see," exclaimed Monty, who did not see at all. "But I'm not one of the moonin' kind, ma'am, an' I'll stick."

"All right. It's only fair, though, to tell you there's a risk. The young fellow doesn't live who can seem to let Rebecca alone. If he could he'd be a godsend to a distracted old woman."

Monty wagged his bare head thoughtfully and slid the brim of his sombrero through his fingers. "Wal, I reckon I've been most everythin' but a gawdsend, an' I'd shore like to try thet."

"What's your name?" she asked with those searching gray eyes on him.

"Monty Bellew, Smoke fer short, an' it's shore shameful well known in some parts of Arizona."

"Any folks living?"

"Yes, back in Iowa. Father an' mother gettin' along in years now. An' a kid sister growed up."

"You send them money every month, of course?"

Monty hung his head. "Wal, fact is, not so reg'lar as

I used to. . . . Late years times have been hard fer me."

"Hard nothing! You've drifted into hard ways. Shiftless, drinking, gambling, shooting cowhand— now, haven't you been just that?"

"I'm sorry, ma'am—I—I reckon I have."

"You ought to be ashamed. I know boys. I raised nine. It's time you were turning over a new leaf. Suppose we begin by burying that name Monty Bellew."

"I'm shore willin' an' grateful, ma'am."

"Then it's settled. Tend to your horse. You can have the little cabin there under the big cottonwood. We've kept that for our hired help, but it hasn't been occupied much lately."

She left Monty then and returned to the ranch house. And he stood a moment irresolute. What a balance was struck there! Presently he slipped saddle and bridle off the horse, and turned him into the pasture. "Baldy, look at thet alfalfa," he said. Weary as Baldy was he lay down and rolled and rolled.

Monty carried his equipment to the tiny porch of the cabin under the huge cottonwood. He removed his saddlebags, which contained the meager sum of his possessions. Then he flopped down on a bench.

"Doggone it!" he muttered. His senses seemed to be playing with him. The leaves rustled above and the white cottonseeds floated down; the bees were murmuring; water tinkled softly beyond the porch; somewhere a bell on a sheep or calf broke the stillness. Monty had never felt such peace and tranquillity, and his soul took on a burden of gratitude.

Suddenly a clear, resonant voice called out from the house. "Ma, what's the name of our new hand?"

"Ask him, Rebecca. I forgot to," replied the mother.

"If that isn't like you!"

Monty was on his way to the house and soon hove in sight of the young woman on the porch. His heart thrilled as he saw her. And he made himself some deep, wild promises.

"Hey, cowboy. What's your name?" she called.

"Sam," he called back.

"Sam what?"

"Sam Hill."

"For the land's sake! . . . That's not your name."

"Call me Land's Sake, if you like it better."

"*I* like it?" She nodded her curly head sagely, and she regarded Monty with a certainty that made him vow to upset her calculations or die in the attempt. She handed him down a bucket. "Can you milk a cow?"

"I never saw my equal as a milker," asserted Monty.

"In that case I won't have to help," she replied. "But I'll go with you to drive in the cows."

~ 2 ~

FROM THAT HOUR DATED MONTY'S APPARENT SUB-jection. HE accepted himself at Rebecca's valuation—that of a very small hired boy. Monty believed he had a way with girls, but evidently that way had never been tried upon this imperious young Mormon miss.

Monty made good his boast about being a master hand at the milking of cows. He surprised Rebecca, though she did not guess that he was aware of it. For the rest, Monty never looked at her when she was looking, never addressed her, never gave her the slightest hint that he was even conscious of her sex.

Now he knew perfectly well that his appearance did not tally with this domesticated kind of a cowboy. She realized it and was puzzled, but evidently he was a novelty to her. At first Monty sensed the usual slight antagonism of the Mormon against the gentile, but in the case of Mrs. Keetch he never noticed this at all, and less and less from the girl.

The feeling of being in some sort of trance persisted with Monty, and he could not account for it, unless it was the charm of this lonely Canyon Walls Ranch, combined with the singular attraction of its young mistress. Monty had not been there three days before he realized that sooner or later he would fall, and great would be the fall thereof. But his sincere and ever-growing admiration for the Widow Keetch held him true to his promise. It would not hurt him to have a terrible case over Rebecca, and he resigned himself to his fate. Nothing could come of it, except perhaps to chasten him. Certainly he would never let her dream of such a thing. All the same, she just gradually and imperceptibly grew on Monty. There was nothing strange in this. Wherever Monty had ridden there had always been some girl who had done something to his heart. She might be a fright—a lanky, slab-sided, red-headed country girl—but that had made no difference. His comrades had called him Smoke Bellew, because of his propensity for raising so much smoke where there was not even any fire.

Sunday brought a change at the Keetch household. Rebecca appeared in a white dress and Monty caught his breath. He worshiped from a safe distance through the leaves. Presently a two-seated buckboard drove up to the ranch house, and Rebecca lost no time climbing in with the young people. They drove off, probably to church at the village of White Sage, some half dozen miles across the line. Monty thought it odd that Mrs. Keetch did not go.

There had been many a time in Monty's life when the loneliness and solitude of these dreaming canyon walls might have been maddening. But Monty found strange ease and solace here. He had entered upon a new era in his life. He hated to think that it might not last. But it would last if the shadow of the past did not fall on Canyon Walls.

At one o'clock Rebecca returned with her friends in the buckboard. And presently Monty was summoned to dinner, by no less than Mrs. Keetch's trenchant call. He had not anticipated this, but he brushed and brightened himself up a bit, and proceeded to the house. Mrs. Keetch met him as he mounted the porch steps. "Folks," she announced, "this is our new man, Sam Hill. . . . Sam, meet Lucy Card and her brother Joe, and Hal Stacey."

Monty bowed, and took the seat assigned to him by Mrs. Keetch. She was beaming, and the dinner table fairly groaned with the load of good things to eat. Monty defeated an overwhelming desire to look at Rebecca. In a moment he saw that the embarrassment under which he was laboring was silly. These Mormon young people were quiet, friendly, and far from curious. His presence at Widow Keetch's table was more natural to them than it seemed to him. Presently he was at ease and dared to glance across the table. Rebecca was radiant. How had it come that he had not observed her beauty before? She appeared like a gorgeous opening rose. Monty did not risk a second glance and he thought that he ought to go far up the canyon and crawl into a hole. Nevertheless, he enjoyed the dinner and did ample justice to it.

After dinner more company arrived, mostly on

horseback. Sunday was evidently the Keetches' day at home. Monty made several unobtrusive attempts to escape, once being stopped in his tracks by a single glance from Rebecca, and the other times failing through the widow's watchfulness. He felt that he was very dense not to have noticed sooner how they wished him to feel at home with them. At length, toward evening, Monty left Rebecca to several of her admirers, who outstayed the other visitors, and went off for a sunset stroll under the canyon walls.

Monty did not consider himself exactly a dunce, but he could not interpret clearly the experience of the afternoon. There were, however, some points that he could be sure of. The Widow Keetch had evidently seen better days. She did not cross the Arizona line into Utah. Rebecca was waited upon by a host of Mormons, to whom she appeared imperiously indifferent one moment and alluringly coy the next. She was a spoiled girl, Monty decided. He had not been able to discover the slightest curiosity or antagonism toward him in these visitors, and as they were all Mormons and he was a gentile, it changed some preconceived ideas of his.

Next morning the new hand plunged into the endless work that needed to be done about the ranch. He doubled the amount of water in the irrigation ditches, to Widow Keetch's delight. And that day passed as if by magic. It did not end, however, without Rebecca crossing Monty's trail, and it earned for him a very pleasant compliment from her, anent the fact that he might develop into a real good milkman.

The days flew by and another Sunday came, very like the first one, and that brought the month of June around. Thereafter the weeks were as short as days. Monty was amazed to see what a diversity of tasks he could put an efficient hand to. But, then, he had seen quite a good deal of ranch service in his time, aside from driving cattle. And it so happened that here was an ideal farm awaiting development, and he put his heart and soul into the task. The summer was hot, especially in the afternoon under the reflected heat from the canyon walls. He had cut alfalfa several times. And the harvest of fruit and grain was at hand. There were pumpkins so large that Monty could scarcely roll one over; bunches of grapes longer than his arm; great luscious peaches that shone like gold in the sunlight, and other farm products of proportionate size.

The womenfolk spent days putting up preserves, pickles, fruit. Monty used to go out of his way to smell the fragrant wood fire in the back yard under the cottonwoods, where the big brass kettle steamed with peach butter. "I'll shore eat myself to death when winter comes," he said.

Among the young men who paid court to Rebecca were two brothers, Wade and Eben Tyler, lean-faced, still-eyed young Mormons who were wild-horse hunters. The whole southern end of Utah was overrun by droves of wild horses, and according to some of the pioneers they were becoming a menace to the range. The Tylers took such a liking to Monty, the Keetches' new hand, that they asked Mrs. Keetch to let him go with them on a hunt in October, over in what they called the Siwash. The widow was prevailed upon to give her consent, stipulating that Monty should fetch back a supply of venison. And Rebecca said she would allow him to go if he brought her one of the wild mustangs with a long mane and a tail that touched the ground.

So when October rolled around, Monty rode off with the brothers, and three days' riding brought them to the edge of a wooded region called the Buckskin Forest. It took a whole day to ride through the magnificent spruces and pines to reach the rim of the canyon. Here Monty found the wildest and most wonderful country he had ever seen. The Siwash was a rough section where the breaks in the rim afforded retreat for the thousands of deer and wild horses, as well as the cougars that preyed upon them. Monty had the hunt of his life, and by the time these fleeting weeks were over, he and the Tylers were fast friends.

Monty returned to Canyon Walls Ranch, pleased to find that he had been sorely needed and missed by the Keetches, and he was keen to have a go at his work again. Gradually he thought less and less of that Arizona escapade which had made him a fugitive. A little time spent in that wild country had a tendency to make past things appear dim and faraway. He ceased to start whenever he saw strange riders coming up the canyon gateway. Mormon sheepmen and cattlemen, when in the vicinity of Canyon Walls, always paid the Keetches a visit. Still Monty never ceased to pack a gun, a fact that Mrs. Keetch often mentioned. Monty said it was just a habit that he hadn't gotten over from his cattle-driving days.

He went to work clearing the upper end of the canyon. The cottonwood, scrub oak, and brush were as thick as a jungle. But day by day the tangle was mowed down under the sweep of Monty's ax. In his boyhood on the Iowa farm he had been a rail splitter. How many useful things were coming back to him! Every day Rebecca or Mrs. Keetch or the boy, Randy, who helped at chores, drove up in the big go-devil and hauled firewood. And when the winter's wood, with plenty to spare, had been stored away, Mrs. Keetch pointed with satisfaction to a considerable saving of money.

The leaves did not change color until late in November, and then they dropped reluctantly, as if not sure that winter could actually come to Canyon Walls this year. Monty even began to doubt that it would. But frosty mornings did come, and soon thin skims of ice formed on the still pools. Sometimes when he rode out of the canyon gateway on the desert, he could see the white line reaching down from the Buckskin, and Mt. Trumbull was wearing its crown of snow. But no real winter came to the canyon. The gleaming walls seemed to have absorbed enough of the summer sun to carry over. Every hour of daylight found Monty outdoors at one of the tasks which multiplied under his eye. After supper he would sit before the little stone fireplace he had built in his cabin, and watch the flames, and wonder about himself and how long this interlude could last. He began to wonder why it could not last always; and he went so far in his calculation as to say that a debt paid fully canceled even the acquiring of a few cattle not his own, in that past which receded ever farther over time's horizon. After all, he had been just a wild, irresponsible cowboy, urged on by drink and a need of money. At first he had asked only that it be forgotten and buried; but now he began to think he wanted to square that debt.

The winter passed, and Monty's labors had opened up almost as many new acres as had been cleared originally. Canyon Walls Ranch now took the eye of Andrew Boller, who made Widow Keetch a substantial offer for it. Mrs. Keetch laughed her refusal, and the remark she made to Boller mystified Monty for many a day. It was something about Canyon Walls someday being as great a ranch as that one of which the church had deprived her!

Monty asked Wade Tyler what the widow had meant, and Wade replied that he had once heard how John Keetch had owed the bishop a sum of money, and that the great ranch, after Keetch's death, had been confiscated. But that was one of the few questions Monty never asked Mrs. Keetch. The complexity and mystery of the Mormon Church did not interest him. It had been a shock, however, to find that two of Mrs. Keetch's Sunday callers, openly courting Rebecca's hand, already had wives. "By golly, I ought to marry her myself," declared Monty with heat, as he thought beside his fire, and then he laughed at his conceit. He was only Rebecca's hired help.

How good it was to see the green burst out again upon the cottonwoods, and the pink on the peach trees! Monty had now been at Canyon Walls a full year. It seemed incredible to him. It was the longest spell he had ever remained in one spot. He could see a vast change in the ranch. And what greater transformation had that labor wrought in him!

"Sam, we're going to need help this spring," said Mrs. Keetch one morning. "We'll want a couple of men and a teamster—a new wagon."

"Wal, we shore need aplenty," drawled Monty, "an' I reckon we'd better think hard."

"This ranch is overflowing with milk and honey. Sam, you've made it blossom. We must make some kind of a deal. I've wanted to speak to you before, but you always put me off. We ought to be partners."

"There ain't any hurry, ma'am," replied Monty. "I'm happy heah, an' powerful set on makin' the ranch a goin' concern. Funny no farmer heahabouts ever saw its possibilities afore. Wal, thet's our good luck."

"Boller wants my whole alfalfa cut this year," continued Mrs. Keetch. "Saunders, a big cattleman, no Mormon by the way, is ranging south. And Boller wants to gobble all the feed. How much alfalfa will we be able to cut this year?"

"Countin' the new acreage, upward of two hundred tons."

"Sam Hill!" she cried incredulously.

"Wal, you needn't Sam Hill me. I get enough of thet from Rebecca. But you can gamble on the ranch from now on. We have the soil an' the sunshine—twice as much an' twice as hot as them farmers out in the open. An' we have water. Lady, we're goin' to grow things on the Canyon Wall."

"It's a dispensation of the Lord," she exclaimed fervently.

"Wal, I don't know about thet, but I can guarantee results. We start some new angles this spring. There's a side canyon up heah thet I cleared. Jist the place fer hogs. You know what a waste of fruit there was last fall. We'll not waste anythin' from now on. We can raise feed enough to pack this canyon solid with turkeys, chickens, an' hogs."

"Sam, you're a wizard, and the Lord surely guided me that day I took you on," replied Mrs. Keetch. "We're independent now and I see prosperity ahead. When Andrew Boller offered to buy this ranch I saw the handwriting on the wall."

"You bet. An' the ranch is worth twice what he offered."

"Sam, I've been an outcast too, in a way, but this will sweeten my cup."

"Wal, ma'am, you never made me no confidences, but I always took you fer the happiest woman I ever seen," declared Monty stoutly.

At this juncture Rebecca Keetch, who had been listening thoughtfully to the talk, as was her habit, spoke feelingly: "Ma, I want a lot of new dresses. I haven't a decent rag to my back. And look there!" She stuck out a shapely foot, bursting from an old shoe. "I want to go to Salt Lake City and buy some things. And if we're not poor any more—"

"My dear daughter, *I* cannot go to Salt Lake," interrupted the mother, a tone of sadness in her voice.

"But I can. Sue Tyler is going with her mother," burst out Rebecca eagerly. "Why can't I go with them?"

"Of course, daughter, you must have clothes to wear. And I have long thought of that. But to go to Salt Lake! . . . I don't know. It worries me. . . . Sam, what do you think of Rebecca's idea?"

"Which one?" asked Monty.

"About going to Salt Lake to buy clothes."

"Perfickly redic'lous," replied Monty blandly.

"Why?" flashed Rebecca, turning upon him with her great eyes aflame.

"Wal, you don't need no clothes in the fust place—"

"Don't I?" demanded Rebecca hotly. "You bet I don't need any clothes for *you*. You never even look at me. I could go around here positively stark naked and you'd never even see me."

"An' in the second place," continued Monty, with a wholly assumed imperturbability, "you're too young an' too crazy about boys to go on sech a long journey alone."

"Daughter, I—I think Sam is right," said Rebecca's mother.

"I'm eighteen years old," cried Rebecca. "And I wouldn't be going alone."

"Sam means you should have a man with you."

Rebecca stood for a moment in speechless rage, then she broke down. "Why doesn't the damn fool— offer to take me—then?"

"Rebecca!" cried Mrs. Keetch, horrified.

Monty meanwhile had been undergoing a remarkable transformation.

"Lady, if I was her dad—"

"But you're—not," sobbed Rebecca.

"Shore it's lucky fer you I'm not. For I'd spank some sense into you. . . . But I was goin' to say I'd drive you back from Kanab. You could go that far with the Tylers."

"There, daughter. . . . And maybe next year you *could* go to Salt Lake," added Mrs. Keetch consolingly.

Rebecca accepted the miserable compromise, but it was an acceptance she did not care for, as was made plain to Monty by the dark look she gave him as she flounced away.

"Oh, dear," sighed Mrs. Keetch. "Rebecca is a good girl. But nowadays she often flares up like that. And lately she has been acting queer. If she'd only set her heart on some man!"

～ 3 ～

MONTY HAD HIS DOUBTS ABOUT THE VENTURE TO which he had committed himself. But he undertook it willingly enough, because Mrs. Keetch was obviously so pleased and relieved. She evidently feared for this high-spirited girl. And so it turned out that Rebecca rode as far as Kanab with the Tylers, with the understanding that she would return in Monty's wagon.

The drive took Monty all day and there was a good deal of upgrade in the rode. He did not believe he could make the thirty miles back in daylight hours, unless he got a very early start. And he just about knew he never could get Rebecca Keetch to leave Kanab before dawn. Still the whole prospect was one that offered adventure, and much of Monty's old devil-may-care spirit seemed roused to meet it.

He camped on the edge of town, and next morning

drove in and left the old wagon at a blacksmith shop for needed repairs. The four horses were turned into pasture. Then Monty went about executing Mrs. Keetch's instructions, which had to do with engaging helpers and making numerous purchases. That evening saw a big, brand-new shiny wagon at the blacksmith shop, packed full of flour, grain, hardware, supplies, harness, and whatnot. The genial storekeeper who waited upon Monty averred that Mrs. Keetch must have had her inheritance returned to her. All the Mormons had taken a kindly interest in Monty and his work at Canyon Walls, which had become the talk all over the range. They were likable men, except for a few gray-whiskered old patriarchs who belonged to another day. Monty did not miss seeing several pretty Mormon girls; and their notice of him pleased him immensely, especially when Rebecca happened to be around to see.

Monty seemed to run into her every time he entered a store. She spent all the money she had saved up, and all her mother had given her, and she even borrowed the last few dollars he had in his pockets.

"Shore, you're welcome," said Monty in reply to her thanks. "But ain't you losin' your haid a little?"

"Well, so long's I don't lose it over *you,* what do you care?" she retorted, saucily, with another of those dark glances which had mystified him before.

Monty replied that her mother had expressly forbidden her to go into debt for anything.

"Don't you try to boss me, Sam Hill," she warned, but she was still too happy to be really angry.

"Rebecca, I don't care two bits what you do," said Monty shortly.

"Oh, don't you?—Thanks! You're always flattering me," she returned mockingly.

It struck Monty then that she knew something about him or about herself which he did not share.

"We'll be leavin' before sunup," he added briefly. "You'd better let me have all your bundles so I can take them out to the wagon an' pack them tonight."

Rebecca demurred, but would not give a reason, which could only have been because she wanted to gloat over her purchases. Monty finally prevailed upon her; and it took two trips for him and a boy he had hired to carry the stuff out to the blacksmith's shop.

"Lord, if it should rain!" said Monty, remembering that he had no extra tarpaulin. So he went back to the store and got one, and hid it, with the idea of having fun with Rebecca in case a storm threatened on the way back to the ranch.

After supper Rebecca drove out to Monty's camp with some friends.

"I don't care for your camping out like this. You should have gone to the inn," she said loftily.

"Wal, I'm used to campin'," he drawled.

"Sam, they're giving a dance for me tonight," announced Rebecca.

"Fine. Then you needn't go to bed atall, an' we can get an early start."

The young people with Rebecca shouted with laughter, and she looked dubious.

"Can't we stay over another day?"

"I should smile we cain't," retorted Monty with unusual force. "An' if we don't get an early start we'll never reach home tomorrow. So you jist come along heah, young lady, about four o'clock."

"In the morning?"

"In the mawnin'. I'll have some breakfast fer you."

It was noticeable that Rebecca made no rash promises. Monty rather wanted to give in to her—she was so happy and gay—but he remembered his obligations to Mrs. Keetch, and remained firm.

As they drove off Monty's sharp ears caught Rebecca complaining—"and I can't do a solitary thing with that stubborn Arizona cowpuncher."

This rather pleased Monty, as it gave him distinction, and was proof that he had not yet betrayed himself to Rebecca. He would proceed on these lines.

That night he did a remarkable thing, for him. He found out where the dance was being held, and peered through a window to see Rebecca in all her glory. He did not miss, however, the fact that she did not appear to outshine several other young women there. Monty stifled a yearning that had not bothered him for a long time. "Doggone it! I ain't no old gaffer. I could dance the socks off some of them Mormons." He became aware presently that between dances some of the young Mormon men came outdoors and indulged in desultory fist fights. He could not see any real reason for these encounters, and it amused him. "Gosh, I wonder if thet is jist a habit with these hombres. Fact is, though, there's shore not enough girls to go round. . . . Holy mackerel, how I'd like to have my old dancin' pards heah! Wouldn't we wade through thet corral! . . . I wonder what's become of Slim an' Cuppy, an' if they ever think of me. Doggone!"

Monty sighed and returned to camp. He was up before daylight, but did not appear to be in any rush. He had a premonition what to expect. Day broke and the sun tipped the low desert in the east, while Monty leisurely got breakfast. He kept an eye on the lookout for Rebecca. The new boy, Jake, arrived with shiny face, and later one of the men engaged by Mrs. Keetch came. Monty had the two teams fetched in from pasture, and hitched up. It was just as well that he had to wait for Rebecca, because the new harness did not fit and required skilled adjustment, but he was not going to tell her that. The longer she made him wait the longer would be the scolding she would get.

About nine o'clock she arrived in a very much overloaded buckboard. She was gay of attire and face, and so happy that Monty, had he been sincere with himself, could never have reproved her. But he did it, very sharply, and made her look like a chidden child before her friends. This reacted upon Monty so pleasurably that he began afresh. But this was a mistake.

"Yah! Yah! Yah!" she cried. And her friends let out a roar of merriment.

"Becky, you shore have a tiptop chaperon," remarked one frank-faced Mormon boy. And other remarks were not wanting to convey the hint that at least one young rider in the world had not succumbed to Rebecca's charms.

"Where am I going to ride?" she asked curtly.

Monty indicated the high driver's seat. "Onless you'd rather ride with them two new hands in the old wagon."

Rebecca scorned to argue with Monty, but climbed quickly to the lofty perch.

"Girls, it's nearer heaven than I've ever been yet," she called gayly.

"Just what do you mean, Becky?" replied a pretty girl with roguish eyes. "So high up—or because—"

"Go along with you," interrupted Rebecca with a blush. "You think of nothing but men. I wish you had . . . but good-by—good-bye. I've had a lovely time."

Monty clambered to the driver's seat, and followed the other wagon out of town, down into the desert. Rebecca appeared to want to talk.

"Oh, it was a wonderful change! I had a grand time. But I'm glad you wouldn't let me go to Salt Lake. It'd have ruined me, Sam."

Monty felt subtly flattered, but he chose to remain aloof and disapproving.

"Nope. Hardly that. You was ruined long ago, Miss Rebecca," he drawled.

"Don't call me miss," she flashed. "And see here, Sam Hill—do you hate us Mormons?"

"I shore don't. I like all the Mormons I've met. They're jist fine. An' your ma is the best woman I ever knew."

"Then I'm the only Mormon you've no use for," she retorted with bitterness. "Don't deny it. I'd rather you didn't add falsehood to your—your other faults. It's a pity, though, that we can't get along. Mother depends on you now. You've certainly pulled us out of a hole. And I—I'd like you—if you'd let me. But you always make me out a wicked, spoiled girl. Which I'm not. . . . Why couldn't you come to the dance last night? They wanted you. Those girls were eager to meet you."

"I wasn't asked—not thet I'd of come anyhow," stammered Monty.

"You know perfectly well that in a Mormon town or home you are always welcome," she said. "What did you want? Would you have had me stick my finger in the top hole of your vest and look up at you like a dying duck and say, 'Sam, please come'?"

"My Gawd, no. I never dreamed of wantin' you to do anythin'," replied Monty hurriedly. He was getting beyond his depth here, and began to doubt his ability to say the right things.

"*Why* not? Am I so hideous? Aren't I a human being? A *girl?*" she asked with resentful fire.

Monty deliberated a moment, as much to recover his scattered wits as to make an adequate reply.

"Wal, you shore are a live human critter. An' as handsome as any gurl I ever seen. But you're spoiled somethin' turrible. You're the most orful flirt I ever watched, an' the way you treat these fine Mormon boys is shore scandalous. You don't know what you want more'n one minnit straight runnin'. An' when you get what you want you're sick of it right away."

"Oh, is that *all?*" she burst out, and then followed with a peal of riotous laughter. But she did not look at him or speak to him again for several long hours.

Monty liked the silence better. He still had the thrill of her presence, without her disturbing chatter. A nucleus of a thought tried to wedge its way into his consciousness—that this girl was not completely indifferent to him. But he squelched it.

At noon they halted in a rocky depression, where water filled the holes, and Rebecca got down to sit in the shade of a cedar.

"I want something to eat," she declared imperiously.

"Sorry, but there ain't nothin'," replied Monty imperturbably, as he mounted to the seat again. The other wagon rolled on, crushing the rocks with its wide tires.

"Are you going to starve me into submission?"

Monty laughed at her. "Wal, I reckon if someone took a willow switch to your bare legs an'—wal, he might get a little submission out of you."

"You're worse than a Mormon," she cried in disgust, as if that was the very depth of depravity.

"Come along, youngster," said Monty with pretended weariness. "If we don't keep steppin' along lively we'll never get home tonight."

"Good! I'll delay you as much as I can. . . . Sam, I'm scared to death to face Mother." And she giggled.

"What about?"

"I went terribly in debt. But I didn't lose my 'haid' as you say. I thought it all out. I won't be going again for ages. And I'll work. It was the change in our fortunes that tempted me."

"Wal, I reckon we can get around tellin' your ma," said Monty lamely.

"You wouldn't give me away, Sam?" she asked in

surprise, with strange intent eyes. And she got up to come over to the wagon.

"No, I wouldn't. Course not. What's more I can lend you the money—presently."

"Thanks, Sam. But I'll tell Mother."

She scrambled up and rode beside him again for miles without speaking. It seemed nothing to Monty to ride in that country and keep silent. The desert was not conducive to conversation. It was so beautiful that talking seemed out of place. Mile after mile of rock and sage, of black ridge and red swale, and always the great landmarks looming as if unattainable. Behind them the Pink Cliffs rose higher the farther they traveled; to their left the long black fringe of the Buckskin gradually sank into obscurity; in front rolled away the colorful desert, an ever-widening bowl that led the gaze to the purple chaos in the distance—that wild region of the riven earth called the canyon country.

Monty did not tell Rebecca that they could not get even halfway home that day, and that they would have to make camp for the night. But eventually, as a snow squall formed over Buckskin, he told her it likely would catch up with them and turn to rain.

"Oh, Sam!" she wailed. "If my things get wet!"

He did not give her any assurance or comfort, and about mid-afternoon, when the road climbed toward a low divide, he saw that they would not miss the storm. But he would make camp at the pines where they could easily weather it.

Before sunset they reached the highest point along the road, from which the spectacle down toward the west made Monty acknowledge that he was gazing at the grandest panorama his enraptured eyes had ever viewed.

Rebecca watched with him, and he could feel her

absorption. Finally she sighed and said, as if to herself, "One reason I'll marry a Mormon—if I have to—is that I never want to leave Utah."

They halted in the pines, low down on the far side of the divide, where a brook brawled merrily, and here the storm, half snow and half rain, caught them. Rebecca was frantic. She did not know where her treasures were packed.

"Oh, Sam, I'll never forgive you!"

"*Me?* What have I got to do about it?" he asked, in pretended astonishment.

"Oh, you *knew* all the time that it would rain," she wailed. "And if you'd been half a man—if you didn't *hate* me so, you—you could have saved my things."

"Wal, if thet's how you feel about it I'll see what I can do," he drawled.

And in a twinkling he jerked out the tarpaulin and spread it over the new wagon where he had carefully packed her cherished belongings. And in the same twinkling her woebegone face changed to joy. Monty thought for a moment that she was going to kiss him and he was scared stiff.

"Ma was right, Sam. You are the wonderfullest man," she said. "But—why didn't you *tell* me?"

"I forgot, I reckon. Now this rain ain't goin' to amount to much. After dark it'll turn off cold. I put some hay in the bottom of the wagon, heah, an' a blanket. So you can sleep comfortable."

"*Sleep!* . . . Sam, you're not going to stop here?"

"Shore am. This new wagon is stiff, an' the other one's heavy loaded. We're blamed lucky to reach this good campin' spot."

"But, Sam, we can't stay here. We must drive on. It doesn't make any difference how *long* we are, so that we keep moving."

"An' kill our horses, an' then not get in. Sorry,

...elayed us five hours we might
...r faster travel in the cool of the

...t to see my reputation ruined?"
...accusing eyes on him.

...ca Keetch, if you don't beat me! I'll
...ss. Where I come from a man can
...desire to spank a crazy gurl without
...ations charged agin him!"

...pank me to your heart's content—but—
...e home first."

...can fix it with your ma, an' I cain't see thet
...to a darn otherwise."

...Mormon girl who stayed out on the desert—
...with a gentile—would be ruined!" she de-

...t we're not alone," yelled Monty, red in the
..."We've got two men and a boy with us."

No Mormon will ever—believe it," sobbed Re-
...cca.

"Wal, then, to hell with the Mormons who won't,"
exclaimed Monty, exasperated beyond endurance.

"Mother will make you marry me," ended Rebecca,
with such tragedy of eye and voice that Monty could
not but believe such a fate would be worse than death
for her.

"Aw, don't distress yourself Miss Keetch," responded Monty with profound dignity. "I couldn't be
druv to marry you—not to save your blasted Mormon
Church—nor the whole damn world of gentiles from—
from conflaggeration!"

~~ 4 ~~

NEXT DAY MONTY DROVE THROUGH WHITE SAGE noon, and reached Canyon Walls about mid-aft noon, completing a journey he would not want undertake again, under like circumstances. He mad haste to unburden himself to his beaming employer.

"Wal, Mrs. Keetch, I done about everythin' as you wanted," he said. "But I couldn't get an early start yestiddy mawnin' an' so we had to camp at the pines."

"Why couldn't you?" she demanded, as if seriously concerned.

"Wal, fer several reasons, particular thet the new harness wouldn't fit."

"You shouldn't have kept Rebecca out all night," said the widow severely.

"I don't know how it could have been avoided," replied Monty mildly. "You wouldn't have had me kill four good horses."

"Did you meet anyone?" she asked.

"Not even a sheepherder."

"Did you stop at White Sage?"

"Only to water, an' we didn't see no one."

"Maybe we can keep the Mormons from finding out," returned Mrs. Keetch with relief. "I'll talk to these new hands. Mormons are close-mouthed when it's to their interest."

"Wal, ma'am, heah's the receipts, an' my notes an' expenditures," added Monty, handing them over.

"My pore haid shore buzzed over all them figgers. But I got the prices you wanted. I found out you gotta stick to a Mormon. But he won't let you buy from no other storekeeper, if he can help it."

"Indeed he won't. . . . Well, daughter, what have you to say for yourself? I expected to see you with the happiest of faces. But you look the way you used to when you stole jam. I hope it wasn't your fault Sam had to keep you all night on the desert."

"Yes, Ma, it was," admitted Rebecca, and though she spoke frankly she plainly feared her mother's displeasure.

"So. And Sam wouldn't tell on you, eh?"

"No, I don't know why he wouldn't! Not out of any feelings for me. . . . Come in, Ma, and let me confess the rest—while I've still got the courage."

Mrs. Keetch looked worried. Monty saw that her anger would be a terrible thing if aroused.

"Ma'am, don't be hard on the gurl," he said, with his easy drawl and smile. "Jist think! She hadn't been to Kanab fer two years. Two years! An' she a growin' gurl. Kanab is some shucks of a town. I was surprised. An' she was jist a kid let loose."

"Sam Hill! So you have fallen into the ranks at last," exclaimed Mrs. Keetch, while Rebecca telegraphed him a grateful glance.

"Lady, I don't savvy about the ranks," replied Monty stiffly. "But I've been falling from grace all my life. Thet's why I'm—"

"No matter," interrupted the widow hastily, and it struck Monty that she did not care to have him confess his shortcomings before Rebecca. "Unpack the wagons and put the things on the porch, except what should go to the barn."

Monty helped the two new employees unpack the old wagon first, and then directed them to the barn.

Then he removed Rebecca's many purchases and piled them on the porch. All the time his ears burned over the heated argument going on within the house. Rebecca seemed to have relapsed into tears while her mother still continued to upbraid her. Monty drove out to the barn considerably disturbed by the sound of the girl's uncontrolled sobbing.

"Doggone! The old lady's hell when she's riled," he thought. "Now I wonder which it was. Rebecca spendin' all her money an' mine, an' this runnin' up bills— or because she made us stay a night out . . . or mebbe it's somethin' I don't know a blamed thing about. . . . Whew, but she laid it onto thet pore kid. Doggone the old Mormon! She'd better not pitch into me."

Supper was late that night and the table was set in the dusk. Mrs. Keetch had regained her composure, but Rebecca's face was woebegone and pallid from weeping. Monty's embarrassment seemed augmented by the fact that she squeezed his hand under the table. But it was a silent meal, soon finished; and while Rebecca reset the table for the new employees, Mrs. Keetch drew Monty aside on the porch. It suited him just as well that dusk was deepening into night.

"I am pleased with the way you carried out my instructions," said Mrs. Keetch. "I could not have done so well. My husband John was never any good in business. You are shrewd, clever, and reliable. If this year's harvest shows anything near what you claim, I can do no less than make you my partner. There is nothing to prevent us from developing another canyon ranch. John had a lien on one west of here. It's bigger than this and uncleared. We could acquire that, if you thought it wise. In fact we could go far. Not that I am money mad, like many Mormons are. But I would like to show them. . . . What do you think about it, Sam?"

"Wal, I agree, 'cept makin' me full pardner seems more'n I deserve. But if the crops turn out big this fall—an' you can gamble on it—I'll make a deal with you fer five years or ten or life."

"Thank you. That is well. It insures comfort in my old age as well as something substantial for my daughter. . . . Sam, do you understand Rebecca?"

"Good Lord, no," exploded Monty.

"I reckoned you didn't. Do you realize that where she is concerned you are wholly unreliable?"

"What do you mean, ma'am?" he asked, thunder-struck.

"She can wind you round her little finger."

"Huh! . . . She jist cain't do anythin' of the sort," declared Monty, trying to appear angry. The old lady might ask a question presently that would be exceed-ingly hard to answer.

"Perhaps you do not know it. That'd be natural. At first I thought you a pretty deep, clever cowboy, one of the devil-with-the-girls kind, and that you would give Rebecca the lesson she deserves. But now I think you a soft-hearted, easy-going, *good* young man, actu-ally stupid when it comes to a girl."

"Aw, thanks, ma'am," replied Monty, most uncom-fortable, and then his natural spirit rebelled. "I never was accounted stupid about gentile gurls."

"Rebecca is no different from any girl. I should think you'd have seen that the Mormon style of court-ship makes her sick. It is too simple, too courteous, too respectful, and too much bordering on the religious to stir her heart. No Mormon will ever get Rebecca, unless I force her to marry him. Which I have been pressed to do and which I hope I shall never do."

"Wal, I respect you fer thet, ma'am," replied Monty feelingly. "But why all this talk about Rebecca? I'm shore mighty sympathetic, but how does it concern me?"

"Sam, I have not a friend in all this land, unless it's you."

"Wal, you can shore gamble on me. If you want I—I'll marry you an' be a dad to this gurl who worries you so."

"Bless your heart! . . . No, I'm too old for that, and I would not see you sacrifice yourself. But, oh, wouldn't that be fun—and revenge?"

"Wal, it'd be heaps of fun," laughed Monty. "But I don't reckon where the revenge would come in."

"Sam, you've given me an idea," spoke up the widow, in a quick whisper. "I'll threaten Rebecca with this. That I could marry you and make you her father. If that doesn't chasten her—then the Lord have mercy upon us."

"She'd laugh at you."

"Yes. But she'll be scared to death. I'll never forget her face one day when she confessed that you claimed she should be switched—well, it must have been sort of shocking, if you said it."

"I shore did, ma'am," he admitted.

"Well, we begin all over again from today," concluded the widow, thoughtfully. "To build anew! Go back to your work and plans. I have the utmost confidence in you. My troubles are easing. But I have not one more word of advice about Rebecca."

"I cain't say as you gave me any advice at all. But mebbe thet's because I'm stupid. Thanks, Mrs. Keetch an' good night."

The painful hour of confused thinking which Monty put in that night, walking in the moonlight shadows under the canyon walls, resulted only in increasing his bewilderment. He ended it by admitting he was now in love with Rebecca, ten thousand times worse than he had ever loved any girl before, and that she could wind him around her little finger all she wanted to. If she knew! But he swore he would never let her find it out.

*　　*　　*

Next day seemed to bring the inauguration of a new regime at Canyon Walls. The ranch had received an impetus, like that given by water run over rich dry ground. Monty's hours were doubly full. Always there was Rebecca, singing on the porch at dusk. "In the gloaming, oh my darling," a song that carried Monty back to home in Iowa, and the zigzag rail fences; or she was at his elbow during the milking hour, an ever-growing task; or in the fields. She could work, that girl; and he told her mother it would not take long for her to earn the money she had squandered in town.

Sunday after Sunday passed, with the usual host of merry callers, and no word was ever spoken of Rebecca having passed a night on the desert with a gentile. So that specter died, except in an occasional mocking look she gave him, which he took to mean that she still could betray herself and him if she took the notion.

In June came the first cutting of alfalfa—fifty acres with an enormous yield. The rich, green, fragrant hay stood knee high. Monty tried to contain himself. But it did seem marvelous that the few simple changes he had made could produce such a rich harvest.

Monty worked late, and a second bell did not deter him. He wanted to finish this last great stack of alfalfa. Then he saw Rebecca running along the trail, calling. Monty let her call. It somehow tickled him, pretending not to hear. So she came out into the field and up to him.

"Sam, are you deaf? Ma rang twice. And then she sent me."

"Wal, I reckon I been feelin' orful good about this alfalfa," he replied.

"Oh, it is lovely. So dark and green—so sweet to smell! . . . Sam, I'll just have to slide down that haystack."

"Don't you dare," called Monty in alarm.

But she ran around to the lower side and presently appeared on top, her face flushed, full of fun and the desire to torment him.

"Please, Rebecca, don't slide down. You'll topple it over, an' I'll have all the work to do over again."

"Sam, I just have to, the way I used to when I was a kid."

"You're a kid right now," he retorted. "An' go back an' get down careful."

She shrieked and let herself go and came sliding down, somewhat at the expense of modesty. Monty knew he was angry, but he feared that he was some other things too.

"There! You see how slick I did it? I could always beat the girls—and boys, too."

"Wal, let thet do," growled Monty.

"Just one more, Sam."

He dropped his pitchfork and made a lunge for her, catching only the air. How quick she was! He controlled an impulse to run after her. Soon she appeared on top again, with something added to her glee.

"Rebecca, if you slide down heah again you'll be sorry," he shouted warningly.

"What'll *you* do?"

"I'll spank you."

"Sam Hill! . . . You wouldn't dare."

"So help me heaven, I will."

She did not in the least believe him, but it was evident that his threat made her project only the more thrilling. There was at least a possibility of excitement.

"Look out. I'm acoming," she cried, with a wild, sweet trill of laughter.

As she slid down Monty leaped to intercept her. A scream escaped from Rebecca, but it was only because of her unruly skirts. That did not deter Monty. He caught her and stopped her high off the ground, and there he pinioned her.

Whatever Monty's intent had been it now escaped him. A winged flame flicked at every fiber of his being. He had her arms spread, and it took all his strength and weight to hold her there, feet off the ground. She was not in the least frightened at this close contact, though a wonderful look of speculation sparkled in her big gray eyes.

"You caught me. Now what?" she said challengingly.

Monty kissed her square on the mouth.

"Oh!" she cried, obviously startled. Then a wave of scarlet rushed up from the rich gold swell of her neck to her forehead. She struggled. "Let me down—you— you gentile cowpuncher!"

Monty kissed her again, longer, harder than before. Then when she tried to scream he stopped her lips again.

"You—little Mormon—devil!" he panted. "This heah—was shore—comin' to you!"

"I'll kill you!"

"Wal, it'll be worth—dyin' fer, I reckon." Then Monty kissed her again and again until she gasped for breath, and when she sagged limp and unresisting into his arms he kissed her cheeks, her eyes, her hair, and like a madman whose hunger had been augmented by what it fed on he went back to her red parted lips.

Suddenly the evening sky appeared to grow dark. A weight carried him down with the girl. The top of the alfalfa stack had slid down upon them. Monty floundered out and dragged Rebecca from under the fragrant mass of hay. She did not move. Her eyes were closed. With trembling hand he brushed the chaff and bits of alfalfa off her white face. But her hair was full of them.

"My Gawd, I've played hob now," he whispered, as the enormity of his offense suddenly dawned upon him. Nevertheless, he felt a tremendous thrill of joy as he looked down at her. Only her lips bore a vestige of color. Suddenly her eyes opened wide. From the sheer glory of them Monty fled.

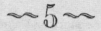

HIS FIRST WILD IMPULSE, AS HE RAN, WAS TO GET OUT of the canyon, away from the incomprehensible forces that had worked such sudden havoc with his life. His second thought was to rush to Mrs. Keetch and confess everything to her, before Rebecca could damn him forever in that good woman's estimation. Then by the time he had reached his cabin and thrown himself on the porch bench, both of these impulses had given place to still others. But it was not Monty's nature to remain helpless for long. Presently he sat up, wringing wet with sweat, and still shaking.

"Aw, what could have come over me?" he breathed hoarsely. And suddenly he realized that nothing so terrible had happened after all. He had been furious with Rebecca and meant to chastise her. But when he held her close and tight, with those challenging eyes and lips right before him, all else except the sweetness of momentary possession had been forgotten. He loved the girl and had not before felt any realization of the full magnitude of his love. He believed that he could explain to Mrs. Keetch, so that she would not drive him away. But of course he would be as dirt under Rebecca's feet from that hour on. Yet even in his mournful acceptance of this fate his spirit rose in wonderment over what this surprising Mormon girl must be thinking of him now.

Darkness had almost set in. Down the lane Monty saw a figure approaching, quite some distance away, and he thought he heard a low voice singing. It could not be Rebecca. Rebecca would be weeping.

"RE-BECCA," called Mrs. Keetch from the porch, in her mellow, far-reaching voice.

"Coming, Ma," replied the girl.

Monty sank into the shadow of his little cabin. He felt small enough to be unseen, but dared not risk it. And he watched in fear and trepidation. Suddenly Rebecca's low contralto voice rang on the quiet sultry air.

> *In the gloaming, Oh my darling!*
> *When the lights are dim and low—*
> *And the quiet shadows falling,*
> *Softly come and softly go.*

Monty's heart swelled almost to bursting. Did she realize the truth and was she mocking him? He was simply flabbergasted. But how the sweet voice filled the canyon and came back in echo from the walls!

Rebecca, entering the square between the orchards and the cottonwoods, gave Monty's cabin a wide berth.

"Isn't Sam with you?" called Mrs. Keetch from the porch.

"Sam? . . . No, he isn't."

"Where is he? Didn't you call him? Supper is getting cold."

"I haven't any idea where Sam is. Last I saw of him he was running like mad," rejoined Rebecca with a giggle.

That giggle saved Monty from a stroke of apoplexy.

"Running? What for?" asked the mother, as Rebecca mounted the porch.

"Ma, it was the funniest thing. I called Sam, but he didn't hear. I went out to tell him supper was ready. He had a great high stack of alfalfa up. Of course I wanted to climb it and slide down. Well, Sam got mad and ordered me not to do any such thing. Then I *had* to do it. Such fun! Sam growled like a bear. Well, I couldn't resist climbing up for another slide. . . . Do you know, Mother, Sam got perfectly furious. He has a terrible temper. He commanded me not to slide off that stack. And when I asked him what he'd do if I did—he declared he'd spank me. Imagine! I only meant to tease him. I wasn't going to slide at all. Then, you can see I *had* to. . . . So I did. . . . I—oh dear!—I fetched the whole top of the stack down on us—and when I got out from under the smothering hay—and could see—there was Sam running for dear life."

"Well, for the land's sake!" exclaimed Mrs. Keetch dubiously, and then she laughed. "You drive the poor fellow wild with your pranks. Rebecca, will you never grow up?"

Whereupon she came out to the porch rail and called, "Sam."

Monty started up, opened his door to let it slam and replied, in what he thought a perfectly normal voice, "Hello?"

"Hurry to supper."

Monty washed his face and hands, brushed his hair, while his mind whirled. Then he sat down bewildered. "Doggone me!—Can you beat thet gurl? She didn't give me away—she didn't lie, yet she never tole. . . . She's not goin' to tell. . . . Must have been funny to her. . . . But shore it's a daid safe bet she never got kissed thet way before. . . . I jist cain't figger her out."

Presently he went to supper and was grateful for the dim light. Still he felt the girl's eyes on him. No doubt she was now appreciating him at last as a real Arizona cowboy. He pretended weariness, and soon hurried away to his cabin, where he spent a night of wakefulness and of conflicting emotions. Remorse, however, had died a natural death after hearing Rebecca's story to her mother.

With dawn came the blessed work into which Monty plunged, finding relief in tasks which kept him away from the ranch house.

For two whole weeks Rebecca did not speak a single word to him. Mrs. Keetch finally noticed the strange silence and reproved her daughter for her attitude.

"Speak to *him?*" asked Rebecca, with a sniff. "Maybe—when he crawls on his knees!"

"But, daughter, he only threatened to spank you. And I'm sure you gave him provocation. You must always forgive. We cannot live at enmity here," she said. "Sam is a good man, and we owe him much."

Then she turned to Monty.

"Sam, you know Rebecca has passed eighteen and she feels an exaggerated sense of her maturity. Perhaps if you'd tell her you were sorry—"

"What about?" asked Monty, when she hesitated.

"Why, about what offended Rebecca."

"Aw, shore. I'm orful sorry," drawled Monty, his keen eyes on the girl. "Turrible sorry—but it's about not sayin' an' doin' *more*—an' then spankin' her to boot."

Mrs. Keetch looked aghast, and when Rebecca ran away from the table hysterical with mirth, the good woman seemed positively nonplused.

"That girl! Why, Sam, I thought she was furious with you. But she's not. It's all sham."

"Wal, I reckon she's riled all right, but it doesn't matter. An' see heah, ma'am," he went on, lowering his voice. "I'm confidin' in you, an' if you give me away—wal, I'll leave the ranch. . . . I reckon you've forgot how once you told me I'd lose my haid over Rebecca. Wal, I've lost it, clean an' plumb an' otherwise. An' sometimes I do queer things. Jist remember thet's why. This won't make no difference. I'm happy heah. Only I want you to understand me."

"Sam Hill!" she whispered in amazement. "So that's what ails you. . . . Now all will be well."

"Wal, I'm glad you think so," replied Monty shortly. "An' I reckon it will be—when I get over these growin' pains."

She leaned toward him. "My son, I understand now. Rebecca has been in love with you for a long time. Just let her alone. All will be well."

Monty gave her one mute, incredulous stare and then he fled. In the darkness of his cabin he persuaded himself of the absurdity of the sentimental Mrs. Keetch's claim. That night he could sleep. But when day came again he found that the havoc had been wrought. He found himself living in a kind of dream, and he was always watching for Rebecca.

Straightway he began to make some discoveries. Gradually she appeared to come out of her icy shell. She worked as usual, and apparently with less discontent, especially in the mornings when she had time to sew on the porch. She would fetch lunch to the men out in the fields. Once or twice Monty saw her on top of a haystack, but he always quickly looked away. She climbed the wall trail; she gathered armloads of wild flowers; she helped where her help was not needed.

On Sunday mornings she went to church at White Sage and in the afternoon entertained callers. But it was noticeable that her Mormon courters grew fewer as the summer advanced. Monty missed in her the gay allure, the open coquetry, the challenge that had once been so marked.

All this was thought-provoking enough for Monty, but nothing to the discovery that Rebecca watched him from afar and from near at hand. Monty could scarcely believe it. Only more proof of his addled brain! However, the eyes which had made Monty Smoke Bellew a great shot and tracker, wonderful out on the range, could not be deceived. When he himself took to spying upon Rebecca, he had learned the staggering truth.

In the mornings and evenings while he was at work near the barn or resting on his porch she watched him, believing herself unseen. She peered from behind her window curtain, through the leaves, above her sewing, from the open doors—from everywhere her great gray hungry eyes sought him. It began to get on Monty's nerves. Did she hate him so much that she was planning some dire revenge? But the eyes that watched him in secret seldom or never met his own any more. Sometimes he would recall Mrs. Keetch's strangely tranquil words, and then he would have to battle fiercely with himself to recover his equanimity. The last asinine thing Smoke Bellew would ever do would be to believe that Rebecca loved him.

One noonday Monty returned to his cabin to find a magical change in his single room. He could not recognize it. Clean and tidy and colorful, it met his eye as he entered. There were Indian rugs on the clay floor, Indian ornaments on the log walls, curtains at his windows, a scarf on his table, and a bright bedspread on his bed. In a little Indian vase on the table stood some stalks of golden daisies and purple asters.

"What happened around heah this mawnin'?" he drawled at meal hour. "My cabin is spruced up fine as a parlor."

"Yes, it does look nice," replied Mrs. Keetch complacently. "Rebecca has had that in mind to do for some time."

"Wal, it was turrible good of her," said Monty.

"Oh, nonsense," returned Rebecca, with a swift

blush. "Ma wanted you to be more comfortable, that's all."

Monty escaped somehow, as he always managed to escape when catastrophe impended. But one August night when the harvest moon rose white and huge above the black canyon rim he felt such a strange impelling presentiment that he could not bear to leave his porch and go into bed. It had been a hard day—one in which the accumulated cut of alfalfa had been heavy. Canyon Walls Ranch, with its soil and water and sun, was beyond doubt a gold mine. All over southern Utah the ranchers were clamoring for that record alfalfa crop.

The hour was late. The light in Rebecca's room had long been out. Frogs and owls and nighthawks had ceased their lonely calls. Only the insects hummed in the melancholy stillness.

A rustle startled Monty. Was it a leaf falling from a cottonwood? A dark form crossed the barred patches of moonlight. Rebecca! She passed close to him as he lounged on the porch steps. Her face flashed white. She ran down the lane and then stopped to look back.

"Doggone! Am I drunk or crazy or just moon-struck?" said Monty rising. "What is the gurl up to? . . . Shore she seen me heah. . . . Shore she did!"

He started down the lane and when he came out of the shadow of the cottonwoods into the moonlight she began to run with the speed of a deer. Monty stalked after her. He was roused now. He would see this thing through. If this was just another of her hoydenish tricks! But there seemed to be something mysterious in this night flight out into the canyon under the full moon.

Monty lost sight of her at the end of the lane. But when he reached it and turned into the field he saw her on the other side, lingering, looking back. He could see her moon-blanched face. She ran on and he followed.

That side of the canyon lay clear in the silver light. On the other the looming canyon wall stood up black, with its level rim moon-fired against the sky. The alfalfa shone bright, and the scent of it in the night air was overpowering in its sweetness.

Rebecca was making for the upper end where that day the alfalfa had been cut. She let Monty gain on her, but at last with a burst of laughter she ran to the huge silver-shining haystack and began to climb it.

Monty did not run: he slowed down. He did not know what was happening to him, but his state seemed to verge upon lunacy. One of his nightmares! He would awaken presently. But there was the white form scrambling up the steep haystack. That afternoon he had finished this mound of alfalfa, with the satisfaction of an artist.

When he reached it Rebecca had not only gained the top, but was lying flat, propped on her elbows. Monty went closer—until he was standing right up against the stack. He could see her distinctly now, scarcely fifteen feet above his head. The moonlight lent her form an air of witchery. But it was the mystery of her eyes that completed the bewitchment of Monty. Why had he followed her? He could do nothing. His former threat was but an idle memory. His anger would not rise. She would make him betray his secret and then, alas! Canyon Walls could no longer be a home for him.

"Howdy, Sam," she said, in a tone that he could not comprehend.

"Rebecca, what you doin' out heah?"

"Isn't it a glorious night?"

"Yes. But you ought to be in your bed. An' you could have watched from your window."

"Oh, no. I had to be out in it. . . . Besides, I wanted to make you follow me."

"Wal, you shore have. I was plumb scared, I reckon. An'—an' I'm glad it was only in fun. . . . But why did you want me to follow you?"

"For one thing, I wanted you to see me climb your new haystack."

"Yes? Wal, I've seen you. So come down now. If your mother should ketch us out heah—"

"And I wanted you to see me slide down *this* one."

As he looked up at her he realized how helpless he was in the hands of this strange girl. He kept staring, not knowing what she would do next.

"And *I* wanted to see—terribly—what you'd do," she went on, with a seriousness that surely must have been mockery.

"Rebecca, honey, I don't aim to do—nothin'," replied Monty almost mournfully.

She got to her knees, and leaned over as if to see more clearly. Then she turned round to sit down and slide to the very edge. Her hands were clutched deep in the alfalfa.

"You won't spank me, Sam?" she asked, in impish glee.

"No. Much as I'd like to—an' as you shore need it—I cain't."

"Bluffer . . . Gentile cowpuncher . . . showing yellow . . . marble-hearted fiend!"

"Not thet last, Rebecca. For all my many faults, not that," he said sadly.

She seemed fighting to let go of something that the mound of alfalfa represented only in symbol. Surely the physical effort for Rebecca to hold her balance there could not account for the look of strain on her body and face. And, in addition, all the mystery of Canyon Walls and the beauty of the night hovered over her.

"Sam, dare me to slide," she taunted.

"No," he retorted grimly.

"Coward!"

"Shore. You hit me on the haid there."

Then ensued a short silence. He could see her quivering. She was moving, almost imperceptibly. Her eyes, magnified by the shadow and light, transfixed Monty.

"Gentile, dare me to slide—into your arms," she cried a little quaveringly.

"Mormon tease! Would you—"

"Dare me!"

"Wal, I dare—you, Rebecca . . . but so help me Gawd I won't answer for the consequences."

Her laugh, like the sweet, wild trill of a night bird, rang out, but this time it was full of joy, of certainty, of surrender. And she let go her hold, to spread wide her arms and come sliding on an avalanche of silver hay down upon him.

～6～

NEXT MORNING MONTY FOUND WORK IN THE FIELDS impossible. He roamed about like a man possessed, and at last went back to the cabin. It was just before the noonday meal. In the ranch house Rebecca hummed a tune while she set the table. Mrs. Keetch sat in her rocker, busy with work on her lap. There was no charged atmosphere. All seemed serene.

Monty responded to the girl's shy glance by taking her hand and leading her up to her mother.

"Ma'am," he began hoarsely, "you've knowed long how my feelin's are for Rebecca. But it seems she— she loves me, too. . . . How thet come about I cain't say. It's shore the wonderfullest thing. . . . Now I ask you—fer Rebecca's sake most—what can be done about this heah trouble?"

"Daughter, is it true?" asked Mrs. Keetch, looking up with serene and smiling face.

"Yes, Mother," replied Rebecca simply.

"You love Sam?"

"Oh, I do."

"Since when?"

"Always, I guess. But I never knew till this June."

"I am very glad, Rebecca," replied the mother, rising to embrace her. "Since you could not or would not love one of your own creed it is well that you love this man who came a stranger to our gates. He is strong, he is true, and what his religion is matters little."

Then she smiled upon Monty. "My son, no man can say what guided your steps to Canyon Walls. But I always felt God's intent in it. You and Rebecca shall marry."

"Oh, Mother," murmured the girl rapturously, and she hid her face.

"Wal, I'm willin' an' happy," stammered Monty. "But I ain't worthy of her, ma'am, an' you know thet old—"

She silenced him. "You must go to White Sage and be married at once."

"At once!—When?" faltered Rebecca.

"Aw, Mrs. Keetch, I—I wouldn't hurry the gurl. Let her have her own time."

"No, why wait? She has been a strange, starved creature. . . . Tomorrow you must take her to be wed, Sam."

"Wal an' good, if Rebecca says so," said Monty with wistful eagerness.

"Yes," she whispered. "Will you go with us, Ma?"

"Yes," suddenly cried Mrs. Keetch, as if inspired. "I will go. I will cross the Utah line once more before I am carried over. . . . But not White Sage. We will go to Kanab. You shall be married by the bishop."

In the excitement and agitation that possessed mother and daughter at that moment, Monty sensed a significance more than just the tremendous importance of impending marriage. Some deep, strong motive was urging Mrs. Keetch to go to Kanab, there to have the bishop marry Rebecca to a gentile. One way or another it did not matter to Monty. He rode in the clouds. He could not believe in his good luck. Never in his life had he touched such happiness as he was experiencing now.

The womenfolk were an hour late in serving lunch, and during the meal the air of vast excitement permeated their every word and action. They could not have tasted the food on their plates.

"Wal, this heah seems like a Sunday," said Monty, after a hasty meal. "I've loafed a lot this mawnin'. But I reckon I'll go back to work now."

"Oh, Sam—don't—when—when we're leaving so soon," remonstrated Rebecca shyly.

"When are we leavin'?"

"Tomorrow—early."

"Wal, I'll get thet alfalfa up anyhow. It might rain, you know. Rebecca, do you reckon you could get up at daylight fer this heah ride?"

"I could stay up all night, Sam."

Mrs. Keetch laughed at them. "There's no rush. We'll start after breakfast, and get to Kanab early enough to make arrangements for the wedding next day. It will give Sam time to buy a respectable suit of clothes to be married in."

"Doggone! I hadn't thought of thet," replied Monty ruefully.

"Sam Hill, you don't marry *me* in a ten-gallon hat, a red shirt and blue overalls, and boots," declared Rebecca.

"How about wearin' my gun?" drawled Monty.

"Your gun!" exclaimed Rebecca.

"Shore. You've forgot how I used to pack it. I might need it there to fight off them Mormons who're so crazy about you."

"Heavens! You leave that gun home."

Next morning when Monty brought the buckboard around, Mrs. Keetch and Rebecca appeared radiant of face, gorgeous of apparel. But for the difference in age anyone might have mistaken the mother for the intended bride.

The drive to Kanab, with fresh horses and light load, took six hours. And the news of the wedding spread over Kanab like wildfire in dry prairie grass. For all Monty's keen eyes he never caught a jealous look, nor did he hear a critical word. That settled with him for all time the status of the Keetches' Mormon friends. The Tyler brothers came into town and made much of the fact that Monty would soon be one of them. And they planned another fall hunt for wild mustangs and deer. This time Monty would surely bring in Rebecca's wild pony. Waking hours sped by and sleeping hours were few. Almost before Monty knew what was happening he was in the presence of the Mormon bishop.

"Will you come into the Mormon Church?" asked the bishop.

"Wal, sir, I cain't be a Mormon," replied Monty in perplexity. "But I shore have respect fer you people an' your Church. I reckon I never had no religion. I can say I'll never stand in Rebecca's way, in anythin' pertainin' to hers."

"In the event she bears you children you will not seek to raise them gentiles?"

"I'd leave thet to Rebecca," replied Monty quietly.

"And the name Sam Hill, by which you are known, is a middle name?"

"Shore, jist a cowboy middle name."

So they were married. Monty feared they would never escape from the many friends and the curious crowd. But at last they were safely in the buckboard, speeding homeward. Monty sat in the front seat alone. Mrs. Keetch and Rebecca occupied the rear seat. The girl's expression of pure happiness touched Monty and made him swear deep in his throat that he would try to deserve her love. Mrs. Keetch had evidently lived through one of the few great events of her life. What dominated her feelings Monty could not divine, but she had the look of a woman who asked no more of life. Somewhere, at some time, a monstrous injustice or wrong had been done the Widow Keetch. Recalling the bishop's strange look at Rebecca—a look of hunger—Monty pondered deeply.

The ride home, being downhill, with a pleasant breeze off the desert, and that wondrous panorama coloring and spreading in the setting sun, seemed all too short for Monty. He drawled to Rebecca, when they reached the portal of Canyon Walls and halted under the gold-leaved cottonwoods: "Wal, wife, heah we are home. But we shore ought to have made thet honeymoon drive a longer one."

That suppertime was the only one in which Monty ever saw the Widow Keetch bow her head and give thanks to the Lord for the salvation of these young people so strangely brought together, for the home overflowing with milk and honey, for the hopeful future.

They had their fifth cutting of alfalfa in September, and it was in the nature of an event. The Tyler boys rode over to help, fetching Sue to visit Rebecca. And there was much merrymaking. Rebecca would climb

111

every mound of alfalfa and slide down screaming her delight. And once she said to Monty, "Young man, you should pray under every haystack you build."

"Ahuh. An' what fer should I pray, Rebecca?" he drawled.

"To give thanks for all this sweet-smelling alfalfa has brought you."

The harvest god smiled on Canyon Walls that autumn. Three wagons plied between Kanab and the ranch for weeks, hauling the produce that could not be used. While Monty went off with the Tyler boys for their hunt in Buckskin Forest, the womenfolk and their guests, and the hired hands applied themselves industriously to the happiest work of the year—preserving all they could of the luscious fruit yield of the season.

Monty came back to a home such as had never been his even in his happiest dreams. Rebecca was incalculably changed, and so happy that Monty trembled as he listened to her sing, as he watched her at work. The mystery never ended for him, not even when she whispered that they might expect a little visitor from the angels next spring. But Monty's last doubt faded, and he gave himself over to work, to his loving young wife, to walks in the dusk under the canyon walls, to a lonely pipe beside his little fireside.

The winter passed, and spring came, doubling all former activities. They had taken over the canyon three miles to the westward, which once cleared of brush and cactus and rock promised well. The problem had been water and Monty solved it by extending a new irrigation ditch from the same brook that watered the home ranch. Good fortune had attended his every venture.

Around the middle of April, when the cottonwoods

began to be tinged with green and the peach trees with pink, Monty began to grow restless about the coming event. It uplifted him one moment, appalled him the next. In that past which seemed so remote to him now, he had snuffed out life. Young, fiery, grim Smoke Bellew! And by some incomprehensible working out of life he was now about to bring life into being.

On the seventeenth of May, some hours after breakfast, he was hurriedly summoned from the fields. His heart appeared to be choking him.

Mrs. Keetch met him at the porch. He scarcely knew her.

"My son, do you remember this date?"

"No," replied Monty wonderingly.

"Two years ago today you came to us. . . . And Rebecca has just borne you a son."

"Aw—my Gawd!—How—how is she, ma'am?" he gasped.

"Both well. We could ask no more. It has all been a visitation of God. . . . Come."

Some days later the important matter of christening the youngster came up.

"Ma wants one of those jaw-breaking Biblical names," said Rebecca pouting. "But I like just plain Sam."

"Wal, it ain't much of a handle fer sech a wonderful little feller."

"It's your name. I love it."

"Rebecca, you kinda forget Sam Hill was jist a—a sort of a middle name. It ain't my real name."

"Oh, yes, I remember now," replied Rebecca, her great eyes lighting. "At Kanab—the bishop asked about Sam Hill. Mother had told him that was your nickname."

"Darlin', I had another nickname once," he said sadly.

113

"So, my man with a mysterious past. And what was that?"

"They called me Smoke."

"How funny! . . . Well, I may be Mrs. Monty Smoke Bellew, according to the law and the Church, but *you*, my husband, will always be Sam Hill to me!"

"An' the boy?" asked Monty enraptured.

"Is Sam Hill, too."

An anxious week passed and then all seemed surely well with the new mother and baby. Monty ceased to tiptoe around. He no longer awoke with a start in the dead of night.

Then one Saturday as he came out on the wide porch, he heard a hallo from someone, and saw four riders coming through the portal. A bolt shot back from a closed door of his memory. Arizona riders! How well he knew the lean faces, the lithe forms, the gun belts, the mettlesome horses!

"Nix, fellers," called the foremost rider, as Monty came slowly out.

An instinct followed by a muscular contraction that had the speed of lightning passed over Monty. Then he realized he packed no gun and was glad. Old habit might have been too strong. His hawk eye saw lean hands drop from hips. A sickening feeling of despair followed his first reaction.

"Howdy, Smoke," drawled the foremost rider.

"Wal, doggone! If it ain't Jim Sneed," returned Monty, as he recognized the sheriff, and he descended the steps to walk out and offer his hand, quick to see the swift, penetrating eyes run over him.

"Shore, it's Jim. I reckoned you'd know me. Hoped you would, as I wasn't too keen about raisin' your smoke."

"Ahuh. What you all doin' over heah, Jim?" asked Monty, with a glance at the three watchful riders.

"Main thing I come over fer was to buy stock fer

Strickland. An' he said if it wasn't out of my way I might fetch you back. Word come thet you'd been seen in Kanab. An' when I made inquiry at White Sage I shore knowed who Sam Hill was."

"I see. Kinda tough it happened to be Strickland. Doggone! My luck jist couldn't last."

"Smoke, you look uncommon fine," said the sheriff with another appraising glance. "You shore haven't been drinkin'. An' I seen fust off you wasn't totin' no gun."

"Thet's all past fer me, Jim."

"Wal, I'll be damned!" exclaimed Sneed, and fumbled for a cigarette. "Bellew, I jist don't savvy."

"Reckon you wouldn't. . . . Jim, I'd like to ask if my name ever got linked up with thet Green Valley deal two years an' more ago?"

"No, it didn't, Smoke, I'm glad to say. Your pards Slim an' Cuppy pulled thet. Slim was killed coverin' Cuppy's escape."

"Ahuh . . . So Slim—wal, wal—" sighed Monty, and paused a moment to gaze into space.

"Smoke, tell me your deal heah," said Sneed.

"Shore. But would you mind comin' indoors?"

"Reckon I wouldn't. But Smoke, I'm still figgerin' you the cowboy."

"Wal, you're way off. Get down an' come in."

Monty led the sheriff into Rebecca's bedroom. She was awake, playing with the baby by her side on the bed.

"Jim, this is my wife an' youngster," said Monty feelingly. "An' Rebecca, this heah is an old friend of mine, Jim Sneed, from Arizona."

That must have been a hard moment for the sheriff—the cordial welcome of the blushing wife, the smiling mite of a baby who was clinging to his finger, the atmosphere of unadulterated joy in the little home.

At any rate, when they went out again to the porch

Sneed wiped his perspiring face and swore at Monty, "—— cowboy, have you gone an' double-crossed thet sweet gurl?"

Monty told him the few salient facts of his romance, and told it with trembling eagerness to be believed.

"So you've turned Mormon?" said the sheriff.

"No, but I'll be true to these women. . . . An' one thing I ask, Sneed. Don't let it be known in White Sage or heah *why* I'm with you. . . . I can send word to my wife I've got to go to Arizona . . . then afterward I'll come back."

"Smoke, I wish I had a stiff drink," replied Sneed. "But I reckon you haven't anythin'?"

"Only water an' milk."

"Good Lawd! For an Arizonian!" Sneed halted at the head of the porch steps and shot out a big hand. His cold eyes had warmed.

"Smoke, may I tell Strickland you'll send him some money now an' then—till thet debt is paid?"

Monty stared and faltered, "Jim—you shore can."

"Fine," returned the sheriff in a loud voice, and he strode down the steps to mount his horse. "Adios, cowboy. Be good to thet little woman."

Monty could not speak. He watched the riders down the lane, out into the road, and through the wide canyon gates to the desert beyond. His heart was full. He thought of Slim and Cuppy, those young firebrand comrades of his range days. He could remember now without terror. He could live once more with his phantoms of the past. He could see lean, lithe Arizona riders come into Canyon Walls, if that event ever chanced again, and be glad of their coming.

avalanche

~~ 1 ~~

NOT MANY YEARS AFTER GENERAL CROOK DROVE
out the last wild remnant of the Apache Indian tribe,
the old Apache trail from the Mogollons across the
Tonto Basin to the Four Peaks country had become a
wagon road for the pioneer cattlemen and sheepmen
who were drifting into the country.

Jacob Dunton and his family made camp one day at
the crossing of the Verde. The country began to have a
captivating look for this Kansas farmer. From the rim
top his keen eyes had sighted a brook meandering
through grassy clearings in the dark green forest below. His wife Jane and Jake, their six-year-old boy,
were tired from the long journey, and a few days' rest
would be good for them. While they recuperated in
camp Jacob rode up toward the rim, finding the magnificent forest, the deep canyons and grassy swales,
the abundance of game, much to his liking.

Upon his return one day he found Jake playing with

a handsome, curly-haired lad, perhaps a year older than himself.

"Hullo, whose kid is thet?" he asked his pioneer wife, who was still young, buxom, and comely.

"I don't know," she replied anxiously. "There have been several wagon trains passing by today. They stopped, of course, for water."

"Reckon this boy got lost an' hasn't been missed yet," replied Dunton. "There'll be someone ridin' back for him."

But no inquiring rider visited the Dunton camp that day, nor the next, nor the day following.

"Jake, what's your new pard's name?" Dunton had inquired of his son.

"I dunno. He won't tell," replied Jake. Name obviously did not matter to this youngster. He was too happy with his playmate to care about superficials.

Mrs. Dunton managed to elicit from the lost boy the name Dodge, but she could not be sure whether that was a family name or one belonging to a place. The lad was exceedingly shy and strange. A most singular thing appeared to be his fear of grown people.

Dunton had decided to homestead in a beautiful valley up the creek, yet he was in no hurry to move. By the wagon trains and travelers who passed his campground he sent on word of the lost boy, Dodge. No one, however, returned to claim him.

"Jane, I've a hunch his people, if he had any, don't want him back," said Dunton seriously to his wife one day.

"Oh, no! Not such a pretty, dear little boy!" she remonstrated.

"Wal, you can never tell. Mebbe he didn't have no folks. I don't know just what to do about it. I cain't go travelin' all over the country lookin' for a lost boy's people. It's gettin' time for me to locate an' run up a cabin."

"We can keep him until somebody does come after him," said Jane. "He an' Jake sure have cottoned to each other. An' you know our Jake was always a stand-offish boy."

"Suits me," replied the pioneer, and forthwith he fashioned a rude sign upon which he cut the words LOST BOY, and an arrow pointing up the creek. This he nailed upon a tree close to where the creek crossed the road. With this duty accomplished he addressed himself to the arduous task of getting his family and outfit up to the site he had chosen for a homestead.

Little Jake called his new playmate Verde, and the name stuck. No anxious father came to claim Verde. In time, and for long after the rude sign had rotted away, the crossing by the road was known as Lost Boy Ford.

The years passed. Ranches began to dot the vast, timbered Tonto Basin, though relatively few in number, owing to the widely scattered bits of arable land with available water. A few settlements, even far more widely separated, sprang up in advantageous places. Wagon trains ceased to roll down over the purple rim and on down through the endless forest to the open country beyond the ranges. The pioneers from the Middle West came no more.

The Tonto remained almost as isolated as before its domain had been invaded. In one way it was as wild as ever it had been in the heyday of Geronimo and his fierce Apaches; and this was because of the rustler bands that found a rendezvous in the almost inaccessible canyons under the rim. They preyed upon the cattlemen and sheepmen, who would have waxed prosperous but for their depredations. Jacob Dunton was one of the ranchers who was kept poor by these cattle-stealing marauders. But despite his losses he could see that the day of the rustler was waning. In fact, the tragic Pleasant Valley War, which was heralded throughout the West as a battle between cattlemen and sheepmen, was really between the ranchers and the rustlers, and it forever broke the stranglehold of the livestock thieves. Slowly the Tonto began to recover, and it began to hold promise for the far future.

Jake and Verde were raised together in a log cabin that nestled under the towering gold and yellow craggy rim. The brook that passed their home roared in spring with the melting snows and sang musically all during the other seasons.

The boys grew up with the deer and the bear and the wild turkeys which ranged their pasture land with the calves and colts. They learned how to track animals as other boys learned to play games. It was to be part of their lives. They hunted and trapped before they even knew how to read. In fact, the few summers' schooling they managed to get did not come until they were between twelve and sixteen years old.

Both of them grew into the rangy, long-limbed type peculiar to the region. The Tonto type was a composite of rider and hunter, wood chopper and calf brander, with perhaps more of the backwoods stamp than that of the range.

Jake, at twenty-two, was a lithe, narrow-hipped, wide-shouldered young giant, six feet tall, with as rugged and homely a face as the bark of one of the pines under which he had grown to manhood. He had a mat of coarse hair, beetling brows, a huge nose, and a wide mouth. But his eyes, if closely looked into, made up for his other possible defects. They were clear gray, intent and piercing, even beautiful in their latent light.

Verde, at twenty-three, was a couple of inches shorter than Jake, a little heavier, yet of the same supple, lithe build, fair and curly-haired, ruddy-cheeked, with eyes of flashing blue, handsome as a young woodland god.

And these two, from the day of their strange meeting at Lost Boy Ford to the years of their manhood, had been inseparable. No real blood brothers could have been closer.

Jake liked hunting best of all work or play, while Verde inclined to horses. Being a born horseman, naturally he gravitated toward riding the range. Jake was the more proficient with rifle and six-shooter, as he was also with everything pertaining to trapping wild animals. Verde had no peer in the use of a lasso. He could rope and throw and tie a steer in record time. Jake's father called Verde the champion "bulldogger" of the Tonto. Verde was not so good with an ax as Jake, but he could mow his way down a field of sorghum far ahead of Jake.

Thus the two of them, with their opposite tastes and abilities, made a team for Jacob Dunton that could not have been equaled in all the Tonto Basin. Long ago Dunton had abandoned any hope of ever learning Verde's parentage. In fact, he did not want to. Verde was as his own son. And Verde had all but forgotten the mystery behind his boyhood. The Duntons had no other children; and the great herd of cattle they hoped to amass someday would belong equally to Jake and Verde.

In spring, after the roundup, which was a long arduous task, owing to the wild timberland and rough canyons where the cattle ranged, there would be the plowing and the planting, the clearing of more land, the building of fences. In the fall would come the harvesting, which time, of all seasons, these back-woods pioneers loved best. They had their husking bees and bean-picking parties and sorghum-cutting rivalries—and their dances, which were the very heart of their lives. In late fall they killed pigs and beeves and deer for their winter meat; and from then on to spring again they chopped wood and toasted their shins before the open fireplace.

During the autumn the settler families on the upper slope of this Tonto Basin gathered once a week for a dance. Occasionally it was held at a ranch cabin, sometimes in the woodland schoolhouse, but mostly in the little town of Tonto Flat.

The dance represented their main social life. They had no church, no county house, no place where old and young could meet. Therefore the dance constituted a most serious and important affair. It was here that the strapping young backwoodsmen met and won their sweethearts. In fact, that was perhaps the vital purpose of the dances. There was little other opportunity for courting.

And seldom did a dance occur without one or more fights, one of which, now and then, could be serious. Fighting was characteristic of the Tonto youths. Had not their fathers fought the rustlers for twenty years? And as these hardy pioneers had settled many feuds over cattle, sheep, land, and water with cold steel or hot lead, so their sons settled many rivalries with brawn and blood.

Jake and Verde went to all the dances. Even when off on a hunt up into the canyons or over the rim, they made sure to get back in time for the great event of the week. And Jake and Verde were very popular among the valley girls. Seldom did they take the same girl twice in one season, and every occasion was a gala one. Sometimes they exchanged girls—an event which was regarded with wonder and amusement by their young comrades, and always with concern by their elders. Jake and Verde were not responding satisfactorily to the real purpose of the dance. Neither youth evinced any abiding interest in any one girl. They were both capital catches for any young woman, and this, coupled with their debonair indifference and their boyish brotherly absorption in each other, was the cause of considerable pique.

"Wal," said Jacob Dunton, "I reckon them thar boys of mine ain't feelin' thar oats yet."

"I'm tellin' you, Pa," replied his wife, "it ain't that. They're both full of fire an' go. It's jist that Jake an' Verde are too wrapped up in each other to see any of these steady home-makin' lasses they meet. I love Jake an' Verde jist as they are, but sometimes it worries me."

"Reckon thar's reason for consarn," said Dunton, shaking his shaggy head. "Some hussy will split them like a wedge in dry pine someday."

~ 2 ~

ONE NIGHT, AT TONTO FLAT, AN EXTRA DANCE WAS given in honor of Miss Kitty Mains, a newcomer to the settlement.

Jake and Verde, learning the news late, arrived without partners when the dance was in full swing. They had ample time to see Miss Mains and watch her before there came any opportunity to meet her. And so even before this meeting took place the havoc had already been wrought.

They also had plenty of time to learn all about her; the information was voluntarily offered by swains as dazzled as they. Kitty was the daughter of a St. Louis horse dealer, who had come to Arizona for his health and who was going to buy out the Stillwell cattle interests and take up ranching on rather a large scale. He was reputed to be rich.

But this news would not have been necessary to excite interest in Kitty Mains. She was strikingly beautiful and something quite new to the gallants of the Tonto Basin. She was small of stature, though graceful and well rounded of form. She had a face that struck men and women alike as pretty and pert, and then gradually grew on one. Her hair was brown, curly, luxuriant, and rebellious. Her small lips, usually curved in a smile, were of the color and sweetness of a ripe cherry. She had a complexion that made the tanned and ruddy skin of the Tonto girls look coarse by comparison. She had an additional advantage over them by being daintily and stylishly dressed, her Eastern gowns showing something of her pretty round arms and white neck. But Kitty's superlative charm lay in her eyes—in the remarkable fact of their variance, for one was blue and the other hazel—and of their strangely contrasting beauty. As it was undoubtedly a fact that Kitty Mains could look at a youth with different kinds of eyes, so it seemed that she could look with two kinds of natures, one sweet, wistful, appealing, and the other a dancing devil.

There was not the slightest doubt that she had heard all about Jake and Verde before they were introduced to her; and very little doubt of her curious and divided interest. No good angel was hovering near these raw and impressionable young men to warn them that Kitty Mains was an unconscious and instinctive flirt, an insatiably greedy little soul who lived on love and had never yet returned it, whose nature would never allow her to brook such a beautiful bond of brotherly affection such as that which long had bound Jake and

Verde so closely together. She had the animal instinct that either garners for herself or destroys.

Out of her multiplicity of partners she found several whom she could exchange or desert for Jake and Verde. So in time they got to dance with her. The other girls present already knew, if Jake and Verde did not know, what had happened.

Kitty was as different to each as were her two eyes and two natures. Verde she tormented with that dancing little demon, tantalizing him, courting him with a running challenge of talk wholly new to him and utterly irresistible, always escaping from his eager arm yet continually drawing him on. Jake she entwined as if she were a clinging vine. She had little to say to this quiet, lonely, backwoods boy. But she gave him that shy, sweet, wistful blue eye, and yielded her soft form to the dance, so that her fragrant hair brushed his lips.

Jake and Verde left the dance in the gray hours of the morning, only when there seemed no more hope to get another dance with Kitty. They rode out under the dark blue dome of sky with its mantle of white stars. They did not feel the nipping, frosty air. They raved and babbled like two silly lads over the charms of the new girl; and always ended with praising the two different eyes—the blue and the hazel—that were so sweet, so strange, so beautiful.

They rode off the highway into the trail through the lonely forest, under the dark pines, and still they talked on, raving over the charms of the new girl from St. Louis, each trying to outdo the other in the extravagance of his praises. But at last they fell silent.

Deeper and higher into the forest land they rode, while the first flush of dawn changed the steely sky to rose over the dark-fringed canyon rim under which they lived. The rose turned to gold, and burst into the rising glory of the sun.

It was like the thing that had as suddenly burst in their own hearts.

All this happened to Jake and Verde along about the end of September, just at the beginning of the golden autumn season.

At first they found time to ride into Tonto Flat together. Then Jake made an excuse to go alone one day, while Verde was off somewhere on the range. When the next dance came around, it was Jake who was the proud escort of Kitty Mains.

Verde did not know what to make of the matter, particularly of his conflicting emotions. It hurt that Jake had not confided in him for the first time in his life. He went to the dance alone, silent and troubled. Kitty gave him more dances than she had reserved for Jake. This was contrary to the custom of the backwoods, for the escort always looked after his partner's dances, and took them all himself if he chose. Jake would have been generous, but he was not permitted to choose, and he found himself lucky to get the few she deigned to give him. Thus it was that Jake had the honor of escorting this captivating and willful damsel, but Verde received most of her dances and the most dazzling of her smiles.

The next week the first rift appeared in the perfect relationship that had existed so long between these more than brothers. They did not yet understand what was taking place. But they did not ride together, nor work, nor hunt together. Verde was gone from home for two days, and returned by way of Tonto Flat, obviously with good reason to be exultant. And it was he who took the bewildering Miss Kitty to the next dance, where his triumph was all too short-lived, for he had to suffer the same treatment she had accorded Jake on the previous occasion.

This triangle affair had now become the talk of the

Tonto Basin. Never had the dances been so largely attended; and a girl would have had to be vain indeed not to be satisfied with Kitty Mains' conquest of the Dunton boys.

They neglected their fall work to such an extent that Dunton took them to task. But his unfamiliar and rude criticism only acted like burning embers upon naked flesh. Mrs. Dunton was too wise to say anything, but she grew more troubled as the days passed. The young men of the Tonto awaited with keen zest and wild speculation the inevitable fight. The young women, aside from natural jealousy and resentment, did not enjoy the strained situation.

Two more dances, one of which Kitty did not attend at all, leaving it a total loss for the lovesick twain, and the other to which she went with young Stillwell, brought matters to a climax between Jake and Verde.

They grew estranged, a feeling which found expression in a desire to be alone rather than in an open break. Their very avoidance of each other's company widened the spiritual gulf that grew wider between them. Because of their long and beautiful companionship, anyone might have imagined that they would talk the matter over in a frank, manly way and decide to go to Kitty together and make her choose between them. But the very intensity of their feelings precluded that. They were in the grip of something beyond their experience.

Everything in the Tonto, according to the old backwoodsmen, presaged one of the long, lingering, late falls. These Indian summer seasons were welcomed by the pioneers. They made preparation for winter less arduous and meant that the winter would be shorter. But sometimes a late fall would end with a terrific storm, and that was always bad. Severe storms up under the rim were liable to destroy much of the improvement accomplished during the summer, not to mention the loss of stock.

The hard frosts did not come; the rains held off; the leaves changed color so slowly that the wonderful golden and scarlet and purple blaze of the canyons did not arrive at its fullness of beauty and fire until toward the end of October. The wild denizens of the forest gave no signs of the approach of winter. Ordinarily the deer and turkeys would be down off the mountain; the acorns would be ripe; the trails would be colorful with fallen leaves; the bears would be fat and "located," as old Dunton would call it. Over all the wilderness lay a drowsy, slumberous sense of waiting. A deep sighing breath soughed through the pine forest. The squirrels delayed their cutting of spruce cones, so that as yet that sure sign of early snows, the thud of dropping cones, did not disturb the peaceful solitude. The elk had not begun to bugle, the jays to squall, the wolves to mourn.

But passion, once awakened in Jake and Verde and at last realized, did not wait for the slow ripening of nature's fruitful season.

No Tonto youths ever let the autumn leaves heap round their long-spurred riding boots in the affairs of heart. They stormed the citadel and were seldom gentle about it. Jake and Verde had magnified in them all the elements of this primitive rock-bounded wilderness. They never rode to Tonto Flat together any more, but there was not one of the closing mellow days of October in which they did not ride to Kitty Mains' door. She found herself caught in her own devious toils. This fierce rivalry between two savage men was something new even to her experience. It frightened her.

For weeks the dances had been held at Tonto Flat and Green Valley, which were more accessible to the majority of Tonto Basin natives than the big log schoolhouse in the forest at the foot of the mountain slope. Here, in the years gone by, had taken place the important dances which had made history for the Tonto; and always the last dance of each season.

November came, with its still, blue-hazed mornings, and its warm, lazy, golden afternoons. But there seemed to be something exciting in the air, a cool breath in the silent forest. The deer had begun to range down from the heights.

Jake and Verde each had long solicited the honor of escorting Kitty Mains to this last dance of the season. In this instance they had given Kitty the privilege of choosing between them. She kept them waiting for her reply. Perhaps it was hard for her to make a decision— to show the Tonto people her preference. Perhaps she could not make up her mind which man she wanted to make happy and which she must hurt. Then perhaps she was afraid of this situation which she herself had brought about. In the end, and late in the day, she refused them both. It was probably the only instance, since her arrival at Tonto Flat, that she showed any strength of character.

On the day of this dance Jake came in from the woods to find Verde sitting aimlessly in the sun out by the log barn.

"Verde," he said, "Kitty sent me word late—she won't go with me tonight."

"Same here, Jake," replied Verde dejectedly.

"She's goin' with Ben Stillwell."

"No!"

"Sure. I heard so this mawnin'."

"Who told you?"

"I was down to the mesa an' dropped in on the Browns. They had all the latest news. Tuck had just come home from town."

"How do you take this snub of Kitty's?"

"Me? I'm not takin' it at all," rejoined Jake darkly.

"Reckon it's sort of a double-jointed slight. Kitty's too smart an' good to hurt one of us."

"I wonder," mused Verde.

"Reckon you savvy how she's upset you an' me?" asked Jake with eyes averted.

"Sure. But she cain't be blamed for that. We only got ourselves to blame."

"Hell of a mess!" mumbled Jake, and stood silent awhile, as if there was much to say, only he did not know what or how. These boys had not thought of each other for weeks. They were almost strangers now.

~3~

THE CHILL, MELANCHOLY TWILIGHT HAD SETTLED down over the Tonto schoolhouse when the first riders and wagons arrived. The November wind moaned through the pines. It bore an ominous note. A low murmur of the swift creek rose from the dark ravine. Voices, a girl's laugh, the crack of iron-shod hoofs on the stone echoed through the forest.

Fires were built, one outside near the great pile of wood cut for this occasion, and another in the stove in one corner of the large, empty barnlike schoolroom. The school benches had been arranged around the walls. Half a dozen lamps emitted an uncertain, dim yellow flare.

Rapidly then the Tonto folk began to arrive, mostly on horseback, but many in wagons, buggies, buckboards. Soon a score or more of riotous children were making merry in the schoolroom. By seven o'clock there were over a hundred folk present, standing, talking, waiting, with more coming all the time.

Every time some newcomers entered the building there would be a stir and a buzz followed by hearty greetings. But when young Stillwell arrived, spick-and-span in his dark suit, and pale with suppressed excitement, leading a slender young woman wrapped in a fur coat, there was sudden cessation of sound.

They were not greeted until they reached the stove, and then a marked constraint seemed to attend the elders at least.

Kitty was cold, and said so in her sweet high treble. Stillwell removed her coat, to disclose her all in white, dainty and alluring, a girl for the backwoodsmen to feast their eyes upon, and over whom the women shook their heads silent and dubious.

But soon the old fiddler arrived with his fiddle, and the dance that would last till daylight was under way. The screaming children, darting among the dancers, were all that kept this annual festivity from being a strange, solemn affair. The young people took their dancing most seriously. There was no shyness, no immodesty, no ranting around, no loud talking, no forwardness; yet a blind man could have sensed that this was a courting business. Round and round the couples swayed in a moving circle, not ungraceful, not without rhythm, the young men with intent look and changeless faces; the girls rapt, absorbed; while the older folk looked on complacently and contentedly and the children played till from sheer exhaustion they fell asleep in the corner behind the stove, where blankets had been laid for them.

Jake and Verde rode down to the harvest dance together, though as uncommunicative as if miles of trail separated them. It was late when they reached the clearing and heard the fiddle and the steady shuffle of many feet. They unsaddled and blanketed their horses. As they approached the big outdoor fire to hold cold hands out to the blaze, the music ceased, and the shuffle of sliding feet changed, and there followed a merry roar of voices. Couples by the dozen emerged from the schoolhouse, some to pause by the fire, and others to wander off under the great solemn pines, close together, holding hands, whispering.

It was Jake who first confronted Kitty, to ask her for a dance. She was flushed, lovely, nervous, yet sincerely glad to see him.

"I've saved three, Jake," she replied, looking up to him with her strange eyes. "One for you and one for Verde—and another for you both to—"

"To fight over, huh?" he drawled. "Well, mebbe it won't come to that. An' Kitty, I'm takin' my dance out in talkin'."

"Oh, no, Jake. That'll spoil the whole evening for me," she pouted.

"Hope not. Anyway it goes."

In due time, when his dance came, Jake unceremoniously drew Kitty away from her admirers, and wrapping her in her coat, he led her out under the white cold stars, into the shadow of the pines. Here he took her little hands and drew her close.

"Kitty, this cain't go on any longer," he said.

"What?" she asked, trying to draw away.

"Why this fast-an'-loose business. . . . You've kissed me, haven't you?"

"Well, no—not exactly," she demurred.

"Yes, you have. Anyway it was enough to let me kiss you—which is a fact as sure as Gawd looks down out of those stars on us. An' you swore you loved me."

"Of course I love you, Jake," she murmured, again her old capricious self, yet as if in earnest for once.

"That's tellin' me again, Kitty dear. That's the fast

of it. But on the other hand you've denied it, flouted me, hurt me. That's the loose of it. . . . Wal, it cain't go on any longer."

"But, Jake, I can't help being myself," she replied rebelliously.

"Reckon I wouldn't have you no different," he went on. "But I love you somethin' turrible, an' if you play any more loose with me—there'll be—I—"

He choked and was silent. Then recovering, he went on in simple, intense eloquence to tell her of his love. She leaned against him, gazing up into his dark face, unresisting, carried away by the intensity of his love, reveling in it, finding in it all that she had yearned for, uplifted and transformed by the urgency and simplicity of his passion.

"An' now, Kitty, with it all told, I can come to somethin' I've never said yet," he ended, with his voice almost a whisper.

"Yes, Jake?" she whispered.

"Are you aimin' to spend the rest of your life here in the Tonto?"

"Why, of course. Father has got back his health. Mother likes the quiet—the green. And I—I love it."

"Then will you marry me?" he asked hoarsely.

"I will, Jake. I—I think I always meant to."

Later in the evening Verde presented himself for the dance that Kitty had promised him. Verde was so different from Jake. She trembled within. How handsome he was, and tonight how white his face and blazing his blue eyes!

"Kit, I reckon I don't care about dancin' this one little dance you've given me."

"Verde, you—you're not very complimentary. I'd love it," she replied, and it was the dancing devil eye that looked at him.

Verde did not ask her to go outdoors. He simply

seized her arm and led the way. And when she demurred about going without her coat he said she would not need it.

"J-Jake and I had—a—an understanding," faltered Kitty.

"Reckon I'm powerful glad," he returned. "You an' I are goin' to have one too."

"Oh!" she exclaimed as he led her, with firm arm under hers, out under the very pine tree where only a short time before she had betrothed herself to Jake. Kitty divined at last that she had been made a victim of her own indiscretion. How could she tell Verde about Jake? Regret and an unfamiliar pang knocked at her heart. She had meant well. These backwoods brothers, this Damon and Pythias twain, had needed a lesson. But something had backfired. Verde was not like Jake, yet how wonderful he was!

"Ver—Verde, I'll freeze out here," she whispered, suddenly aware of the cold and of a chill that had nothing to do with the temperature.

For answer, Verde caught her up off the ground and like a great bear hugged her close to his breast. She could see his white face, radiant and beautiful in the starlight, yet somehow stern. She felt her breast swell against his.

"Kit, darlin', this is our understandin'," he whispered. "I reckon I've always been too easy with you. I never touched you—like this—never kissed you before like I am—"

"Verde, you—you mustn't," she pleaded, trembling in his arms.

He kissed her lips. She cried out in protest, yet with the realization of a tide that she could not, did not, want to resist. But she gazed up at him, wide-eyed, fascinated, struggling to remember something. Her lips were parting to speak when he closed them with kisses, and then her eyes.

"Kit—I love—you so!" he said passionately, hoarsely, lifting his face from hers. "Say you love me . . . or I'll pack you on a hoss—off into the woods."

But Kitty could not speak.

"Say it!" he commanded, shaking her, and he kept it up until she slipped an arm around his neck.

Kitty was in a daze when once more she found herself among the dancers. Her partner, young Stillwell, claimed her, but the dance had become a nightmare. All the gaiety and excitement of the occasion were gone.

The evening wore on toward the inevitable retribution which she knew was in store for her. At midnight a hearty supper was served. It was a hilarious occasion. Kitty's vague fears seemed lost, for the moment, and she was almost herself again. She dared not look at Jake or Verde, yet an almost irresistible longing to do so seized her as she sat on a school bench with young Stillwell.

At last the moment came when both Jake and Verde presented themselves for that third dance one of them was to get. Kitty seemed to sense that the hum of voices had ceased, to know that all the faces in the room were turned upon her, though a wave of terror was causing her to tremble as if from an ague.

"My dance, Kitty," drawled Jake.

"Well, Kit, I reckon this dance is mine," said Verde.

"I—I'll—divide it," she faltered, not looking up.

"Not with me, you won't," retorted Verde, his blue eyes flashing fire.

"Kitty, I hate to say it—but I cain't share this with Verde," said Jake.

"But I didn't promise it to either of you," she barely whispered.

"Not in so many words," returned Jake, attempting to grab her hand.

That was the torch. Verde turned to Jake.

"Are you disputin' my lady friend's word?" he asked belligerently.

"Sure am," replied Jake coolly.

Verde stepped forward and slapped his brother's face, not violently, but with what seemed to be slow deliberation.

With the suddenness of a panther Jake lunged out to knock Verde down. Kitty screamed. The crowd gasped, then fell silent. Slowly Verde raised himself on his elbow. His face was changing quickly from red to white. He stretched up his free arm, and his extended fingers quivered.

"Jake!"

"Get up an' ask the lady's pardon," demanded Jake wildly.

"You hit me!" exclaimed Verde unbelievingly.

"Nope. I just blowed a thistledown at you," replied Jake.

In one single bound Verde was on his feet. Tearing off coat and tie, he confronted the man who had been almost a brother to him. "Come out!" he challenged, his voice hoarse with rage. The circle of startled onlookers parted.

In another moment they stood face to face in the light of the roaring bonfire. The crowd of men and boys, and a few of the girls, had poured out after them.

Then like two mad bulls Jake and Verde rushed at each other. They gave flailing blow for flailing blow. They danced around in the red firelight, seeking an opening to deliver damaging blows that were intended to hurt and to maim. Tonto fights were usually marked by hilarity among the spectators. But there was none here. This was strange, unnatural, hateful—to watch these friends and brothers so deadly, so cold and savage, with murder in their every action.

Their white faces and white shirts soon were

bloody. They fought for a long time, erect and silent, knocking each other down, leaping up and rushing in again. Then they clinched, and wrestling, stumbling, they fell to roll over and over on the ground.

That battle between the Duntons was the worst that had ever been fought at the old schoolhouse. It lasted two hours, and ended with Jake lying unconscious and bedraggled in the mud, and Verde, hideously marked and bloody, staggering to his feet and out into the gloom of the forest.

~~ 4 ~~

JAKE HAD BEEN SO BADLY BEATEN THAT HE WAS IN bed for a week, during which time he saw only his mother. In summer and fall he and Verde always slept in the loft over the porch. But Verde had not been there now for many days.

During this week of pain and shame, Jake's mind had been a numbed thing, dark and set and sinister. He could not think beyond the fact that he had been terribly whipped and disgraced before a crowd of Tonto folk, one of whom had been Kitty Mains. She had seen him stretched in the mud, at the hands of Verde. His battered face burned with the disgrace of it. His scarred fists clenched and unclenched impatiently.

Jake always turned his bruised and beaten face to the wall when his mother climbed the ladder to the loft, bringing food and drink he did not want and which he had to force himself to take. She had ceased her importunities on behalf of Verde. They were useless.

At last Jake crawled down out of his hole, feeling as mean as he knew he looked. He wanted to get away into the woods quickly before anyone saw him! That was the only thought in his mind.

But while he was packing his outfit his father suddenly confronted him.

"Your ma said there ain't no use of talkin' to you," be began gruffly.

"Reckon not," replied Jake, turning away the face he was ashamed to reveal.

"Wal, I'll have a word anyhow," rejoined the father. "From now on is this heah Tonto Basin goin' to be big enough for you an' Verde?"

"Hell no!"

"Ahuh, I reckoned so, an' it's shore a pity," said Dunton sadly.

"Where is Verde?" asked Jake.

"I don't know. He never come home. But he sent word that if you wanted satisfaction you'd know where to find him."

Jake made no reply. A smoldering fire of hatred within him would not let him speak to those who loved him. Old Dunton hung around, lending a hand at his son's packing.

"Wal, I see you're off to set a string of traps," he finally forced himself to say. "It's a plumb good idee. Work's most all done for the fall, an' I can spare you. Mebbe you'll be better for a lonesome trip. Nothin' like the woods to cure a feller of most anythin'. But, Jake, I don't like the look an' feel of the weather. If I don't disremember, it was this way one fall fifteen years ago. No rain. Late frost. Winter holdin' off. But, Lord—when she broke! . . . Washed the cabin away, that storm!"

"It's all one to me, Pa," replied Jake dully. And leading his pack horse, Jake rode away from the ranch without thinking to bid his parents good-by.

The day fitted Jake's mood. The sky was overcast, dull, leaden gray, gloomy and forbidding, with a dim sun showing red in the west. The fall wind mourned through the pines. It was cold and raw, whipping up into gusts at times, then subsiding again. The creek had run so low that now it scarcely made any sound on its way down to the valley. Jake rode out of the pines down into the cedars and oaks and sycamores. In the still pools of water the bronze and yellow leaves floated round and round.

At length Jake reached the junction of the trail with the highway, and soon came to where it crossed the Verde Creek. Lost Boy Ford! He had never forgotten, until these last bitter weeks, the significance of this place. For a few moments a terrific strife warred within him. But he quelled it. Nothing could stand against his jealousy and his shame. Kitty loved him dearest and best, but she must also have loved Verde, or he never would have acted as he had. The Tonto Valley was not large enough for both Verde and him. Who would have to go? That would have to be decided; and as Jake knew that neither he nor Verde would ever relinquish the field to the other, it seemed settled that death must step in for the decision. Jake realized now that he was no match for Verde in the rough and terrible Tonto method of fighting; on the other hand, he knew that in a battle with weapons such as must decide this bitter feud he would kill Verde. And such was the dark and fierce violence to which his passion had mounted that he brooded with savage anticipation over his power to rid himself forever of his rival.

Soon he headed off the road into the thickets of scrub oak and jack pine, manzanita and mescal, and began to climb an old unused trail. It led up over the slope to the mesa, into the cedars and piñons and junipers, and at last into the somber forest again.

Here it was like twilight, cool, still, and lonely. The peace of the wilderness tried to pierce Jake's brooding, bitter thoughts, and for the first time in his life it failed. A monstrous wall of bitterness seemed to enclose him.

He climbed high, riding for miles, in a multitude of detours and zigzags, along a trail thousands of feet above the basin below. The slopes grew exceedingly steep and rough. In many places he dismounted to make his way on foot. How dry the brush and soil! The tufts of grass were sere and brown; the dead manzanita broke off like icicles.

At length he arrived at the base of the rim wall. It towered above, seemingly to the sky. A trail ran along the irregular stone cliff, and there were fresh hoof tracks in it. They had been made by Verde's horse, and were a day or two old, perhaps a little more. If Jake had felt any uncertainty it ended right there. Verde had indeed known where to come to give him satisfaction.

Jake rode on to a corner of the wall. Here the trail plunged down. A mighty amphitheater opened in the rim. It was miles across and extended far back. All around it the capes and escarpments loomed out over the colorful abyss.

It seemed to be a scene of dying fires. The ragged gold of the aspens showed dim against the scarlet maples, the red sumac, the bronze oaks, the magenta gums, and all the dark greens. Yellow crags leaned with their great slabs of rock over the void. Here and there gleamed cliffs of dull pink, with black eyelike caves. Far down in the middle of this gulf there was a dark canyon. Black Gorge!

This was Jake's objective. He gazed down with narrowed eyes, strangely magnifying. Ten years before he and Verde had discovered by accident a way to get down into this almost inaccessible fastness under the rim. They had named it Black Gorge. No other trappers or hunters or riders had ever penetrated it. As boys they had made it their rendezvous, Jake to trap and hunt, Verde to corral his wild horses. They went there several times each year, usually together, but sometimes alone. It grew to mean much to them, and they loved it.

"Verde is down there waitin'," muttered Jake, and the somber shadow that had closed over his mind seemed to come between his eyes and the wonderful beauty of the scene.

A sudden rush of wind, wailing in the niches of the cliff overhead, turned Jake's thoughts to the weather. The habit of observation was strong in him. He gazed down and across the basin. And he was suddenly amazed by the sight he saw.

He had seen all kinds of light and cloud effects over the vast valley below, but never before one of such weird, sinister aspect. The sun was westering over the Mazatzals, and through the dark riven pall of cloud it shed a gleam of angry red. From the southwest a lowering multitude of pale little clouds came scudding toward the rim. They were the heralds of storm. But as yet, except for the moan of the wind along the cliff, there was no sound. The basin lay deep in shadow. The cold gray tones near at hand, the smoky sulphurous red of the sunset, the utter solitude of the scene, the vast saw-toothed gap in the rim wall, the distant forbidding shadow of Black Gorge, the bleak November day that was to mark the end of the lingering autumn, the all-pervading spirit of nature's inevitable and ruthless change from lull to storm, from peace to strife, from the saving and fruitful weeks of the past to the ominous promise of sudden storm and destruction—all these permeated Jake's being, and possessed him utterly, and sent him down the trail deaf at last to a still small voice that had been whispering faintly, yet persistently at the closed door of his heart.

~ 5 ~

THERE WAS ONLY ONE ENTRANCE TO BLACK GORGE that Jake had ever been able to discover. He had found various slopes along its three-mile zigzag length where an Indian or an agile young man might by supreme pluck and exertion climb out. But for the most part it was as unscalable as it was inaccessible. A signal proof of the nature of Black Gorge was the fact that in the late fall only a few deer and no bear frequented it.

While it required hours to climb out by the only trail Jake knew, it took but a short time to make the descent. Without a horse Jake could get down in less than a quarter of an hour. That, however, was practically by sliding down. Now, with saddle and pack horse, Jake had all he could do to keep the three of them together. Finally his saddle horse got ahead. Several times the pack animal slipped; and it was difficult to adjust the ropes and bags on the almost perpendicular slope.

Black Gorge deserved its name. It would have been black even without the somber, fading twilight. The walls of stone were stained dark, and in places where ledges and steps and slopes broke the sheer, perpendicular line, brush and moss and vines mantled them so thickly that they looked black in the gloom. At the lower end of the gorge, where Jake had descended, the stream had no outlet. The creek was dry now, but when water flowed there it merely sank into the jumble of mighty mossy boulders. Once no doubt there had been an outlet, but it had been choked by the fall of a splintered cliff.

Jake mounted to ride up a narrow defile. He was concerned at the moment about the water. Black Gorge had never, to his knowledge, been completely dry. But far up the gorge he knew of a spring that ought still to be alive. Besides, he began to feel a cool misty rain on his face.

At this moment his mind reverted again to Verde. In the gathering gloom he could not see the trail, but he had no doubt about Verde's tracks being there. He almost reined in his horse so he could wait and think what to do. But there was nothing more to be considered on that score. It was settled. When he faced Verde again, there would be need of but few words. The rest would be action. Even so, Jake felt a monstrous hand at the back of him, propelling him toward something that he had gladly and sternly willed, yet against which at odd moments his soul revolted.

The gorge widened, the walls ceased to tower and lean, the slopes slanted up out of sight, and the gray gloom lightened considerably. The trail climbed from the dry stream bed to a bench that soon grew level. Jake heard the clucking of wild turkeys and then the booming flap of heavy wings in the branches of a tree. Toward the upper end this bench held a fine open grove of pines and spruce. Jake saw the dark spear-pointed spruce that towered above the little log cabin he and Verde had built there years ago. So long ago and far away those years seemed now!

Jake's instinct was to dismount and draw a gun. Not to be ambushed or surprised! But he cursed the thought that was so unfamiliar to him.

His expectation was to see the light of a campfire, or a flickering gleam from the door of the cabin, as he had many and many a time beheld with glad eyes. But the familiar space was blank, the cabin dark. Jake dismounted, and throwing his bridle, with slow step went forward. The cabin was deserted. It smelled dry and musty. No fire had been kindled there for a long time. He heard the rustling of mice and felt the wind of bats flying close by his head.

Verde might have come, but he was not there now. Sudden, strange relief swept over Jake. He sank to a seat on the edge of the little porch. His sombrero fell off unheeded, and the cold misty rain touched his face. His heart labored as though after a long strain. He sat there in the lonely, silent gorge, vaguely, dully conscious of an agony deep hidden somewhere under the weight of other emotions. It passed, and he addressed himself to the necessary tasks.

He unsaddled and unpacked, and turned the horses loose, with the thought that it was well for them a storm was brewing. Then he carried his packs and saddle inside the cabin, and set about building a fire in the rude stone fireplace. He appeared slow and awkward. Not only were his fingers all thumbs, but they also trembled in a way quite incomprehensible to him.

"Reckon I'm cold an' hungry," he thought.

Every few moments, while cooking supper, which he quite unconsciously planned for two, he would halt in his preparations and listen for the thud of hoofs or the jangle of spurs. But he heard only the melancholy wail of the rising wind.

Presently he stuck a dry fagot of pitch pine into the fire, and with a blazing torch he went outside the cabin to search in the dust for tracks. He found only his own and those made by his horses. Not satisfied, he made a more thorough search. But it was all in vain!

"Verde hasn't been here," he muttered at last, and pondered the situation. There was absolutely no doubt about the fact of Verde's fresh tracks in the trail above the gorge. What had delayed him? And Jake reminded himself of Verde's impetuosity and recklessness on bad trails.

Jake went back into the cabin, where, as many times before, he set some food and drink to keep hot in case Verde might arrive late. Then he unrolled his bed on the heavy mat of dry spruce boughs. This done, he stepped out again. The darkness was like pitch. High up there along the black rim the wind made a low, dismal roaring sound. He could see the leaden band of sky between the two black rims.

He returned presently to the warm fireside, to which he extended his nervous hands. He faced the fire awhile. That had always been one of his joys. But tonight it was not a joy. An arch face suddenly shone out of the glow—a girl's face, roguish, with sweet red lips and strange, unmatched, inviting eyes. Jake had to turn his back to them.

It struck him singularly that Kitty Mains' face in the embers of this cabin fire was something he had never before beheld there. She was something new. She did not belong to that cabin. Thought of her seemed out of place there. He did not even want to think of her now.

When the fire died low Jake went to bed. He was tired and his eyes were heavy. Sleep at last overcame his mind.

In the night he awoke. A tiny pattering of rain sounded on the roof. The wind had lulled somewhat. The night was so black he could not see the door or window. He could tell that the hour was late, for he had rested. And gradually he grew wide awake. The pattering rain ceased, came again in little gusts, died away, only to return. It recalled to Jake that his father had once forbidden him and Verde to camp very late in the fall at this Black Gorge cabin. A blizzard such as sometimes set in after a late fall might snow them in for the whole winter. Jake had completely forgotten this. Likewise had Verde, or if he had not forgotten, he had come anyway. Black Gorge was the one hiding place where they would not be disturbed. His father knew of it, yet could never have found the way there.

The rain pattered again, slightly harder, and a wind sighed in the pines and spruces over the cabin. Suddenly a low, distant rumble startled Jake. Thunder! He sat up in bed, listening. A thunderclap late in the fall was rare and always preceded a terrible storm. Possibly he was mistaken. Sometimes rocks rolled down in distant canyons, making a sound like thunder.

Slowly Jake settled back in his blankets, his alarm dispelled. The rain grew into a steady low roar. Then it fell away for a while. The night wind lulled again. Silence and blackness lay like weights upon Jake's senses.

Then the ebony darkness split. An appalling white light flashed through the open door. The cabin was illuminated with the brightness of noonday. Outside, the black pines stood up against the blue-white glare, the black jaws of the gorge seemed to be snapping at the angry sky. Then thunder crashed with a deafening blast. The cabin shook. The sharp explosion changed to boom and bellow, filling the narrow gorge with reverberating echoes, endlessly repeated until they rumbled away into utter silence.

Uncertainty ceased for Jake Dunton. The long, late Indian summer, so colorful and mellow and fruitful, must be paid for in the harsh terms with which nature always audited her account in the Tonto. Jake forgot his mission there in the realization that fate had shut him in Black Gorge on the eve of a blizzard. At the moment the peril did not strike him. He reacted as he might have on any of the other numerous sojourns in this canyon. He thought of Verde out there somewhere in the blackness.

"Damn Verde anyhow," complained Jake. "Why won't he ever listen to me?"

The pattering rain commenced again, and this time did not cease. Nor did the wind lull. Both perceptibly augmented, but so slowly as to persuade the lonely listener against his better judgment. They bade him hope against hope.

Then the storm broke with savage and demoniac fury. There was no more thunder, or at least in the mighty roar of wind and water Jake could not distinguish any. It took all Jake's strength to close the cabin door. He went back to bed, thankful for the impervious roof he and Verde had built on that cabin, and for the safe site they had chosen.

His ears became filled with an infernal din. The gorge might have become the battleground of all the elements from the beginning of time. Jake had never experienced such screaming of winds, such a torrential deluge of rain. He lay there, forgetting himself, fearful only for the lost Verde. Verde, the boy—lost again! And each terrible hour the storm gained in strength, changing, swelling, mounting to cataclysmic force.

Toward dawn, which he ascertained by a grayness superseding the pitch blackness, there came a gradual lessening of the deluge and lulls in the bellowing of the wind.

Day broke leaden, gusty, with signs of the inevitable change from rain to snow. Jake struck a fire and then went out to look around.

Well indeed was it that the cabin had been erected on a bench high above the stream bed. Where last night had been a rough boulder and gravel-strewn gully, there was now a lake. What amazed Jake was the fact that he could not note any current. Perhaps it was because of the enormous volume of water that must be draining out of the gorge; and the underground exit was not large enough to take care of it.

Nevertheless, that theory did not wholly satisfy Jake.

Thin yellow sheets of water were falling from the cliffs, and here and there narrow torrents rushed pell-mell down the cracks and defiles of the slopes.

Jake gazed up at the dark, leaden sky. The storm clouds had lodged against the rim and hung there. Only in a few places could he see the ramparts, with the gray wall fringed by black pine. The air was still warm, but a gust of wind now and then brought a cold raw breath. During the day, or more likely when night fell, the rain would turn to snow.

~~ 6 ~~

JAKE WENT INTO THE CABIN TO COOK BREAKFAST. The situation was beyond him. By all the woodcraft of which he was master, he knew that the imperative need was to climb out of the gorge before the snow made it impossible. If it had not been for the certainty of Verde's horse tracks on the trail Jake would have attempted to escape at once. But he well knew that Verde would not leave, even if he were able. Jake had no alternative. How futile now that a few hours of oblivion in sleep had brought his mind back toward normal! The die was cast. The catastrophe of a great storm could not make the situation any more desperate for him and Verde. But it made him think; and he had to deny the reason that began to dispell his passion of the past few weeks.

Methodically Jake went about his preparations for breakfast. He was a good cook and had always taken pride in the accomplishment. His keen sensibilities, however, were wholly absorbed in things outside the cabin—the moan of the wind rising again, the frequent rain squalls, the increasing roar of falling water. With some feeling that he could not understand he did not expect Verde, yet he listened for the sound of hoofs or the jangle of spurs.

He poured a second cup of coffee. Lifting the cup, he was about to drink when something happened wholly new in his experience. He wanted to drink, but could not.

Halfway to his lips the full cup poised.

Jake stared. The coffee was quivering.

"Gosh! Am I that nervous?" he exclaimed, and he set the cup down on a bench.

But the coffee continued to quiver. Indeed, the motion increased. There were queer little circles and waves inside the cup!

"Reckon I'm loco," muttered Jake. Nevertheless, he strained his faculties. Something was wrong. In him, for a certainty, but also outside! He continued to stare at the coffee in the cup. Then he heard the rustling of the dry spruce boughs under his bed. Mice! He thought it rather an odd hour for mice to begin emerging. Next a faint rattling of the loft poles attracted his attention.

The whole cabin was shaking. Jake leaped to his feet, and rushed toward the door. The tremor increased. His cooking utensils began to clatter. The cans on the shelves took to dancing. The earth under the cabin was trembling.

A rumbling sound filled Jake's ears. Thunder! The storm was about to break into its second and most fearful phase. It was a long, low, dull roar, gaining volume at the end instead of dying away! Was that thunder?

"Avalanche!" yelled Jake, and bounded wildly out of the cabin.

In the open he halted. His terror had been absurd. The cabin was so situated that no earth slide or rolling rocks could reach it.

Then his gaze fixed upon the stretch of gorge below. He could see to the narrow passage between the black walls through which he had come last night. Everywhere water was running off the cliffs. The canyon appeared to be wreathed in waterfalls, lacy, thin, yellow, with some like ragged ribbons of water.

The sound that had alarmed Jake did not cease. It grew in intensity. Slides of weathered rock on the slopes above! His keen eye sought the heights.

The skyline of the rim wall had changed. Could it be hidden in cloud? But the gray pall hung above and beyond. There seemed to be movement, either of a drifting veil of rain or a long section of slope. Jake wondered if his eyes were deceiving him. Had his love for Verde and Kitty, the jealousy and the fight and the hate, and the dreadful night of storm unhinged his mind? Was he going crazy?

No! His eagle eye had the truth at last. A section of the rim wall had slipped and was sliding down toward the lower end of Black Gorge.

Jake stood there, motionless and dumb with mingled terror and awe. The section of the rim, with its fringe of black pines erect, was moving downward with a gathering and ponderous momentum. The rumble increased to thunder.

A cloud of yellow dust began to lift against the background of stone wall and leaden sky, quickly blotting them out.

Jake's straining sight recorded what seemed to be an illusion in his stunned mind. The line of erect pine trees turned at right angles, and the black spear-tipped trees pointed out over the gorge. Then they waved and dipped. The line broke, the trees leaned and whirled and fell, to be swallowed up by the sliding slope. Only the thundering, rending roar gave reality to what Jake saw. The section of rim wall, giving way, had started the whole slope below into a colossal avalanche. It was a brain-numbing spectacle! The vast green slope of cedar and piñon, of manzanita and oak, of yellow crag and red earth, had become a swelling, undulating cataract. It was beautiful, awe-inspiring. Only the cataclysmic sound rendered proof of its destructive force.

But in a few more seconds the grace and rhythmic movement gave place to upheaval, and then to a tremendous volleying of boulders flung ahead of the avalanche. Rocks as large as cabins hurdled the narrow split of Black Gorge. Large and small they began to crack like cannon balls against the far wall of the gorge.

Jake could see, at the instant when the green mass reached the verge, the width of canyon light streaked by multitudes of falling rocks. Then the avalanche, like a vast, tumbling waterfall of rocks and debris, slid over to fill the end of the gorge.

A terrific wind, propelled up the canyon, staggered Jake. The roar that had grown awful ceased to be sound. He heard no more.

The lower end of Black Gorge was buried by an avalanche that concealed its crushed and splintered mass of debris under a mantle of dust. The lake that had formed at the lower end of the gorge, and which had been displaced by the avalanche now, came swelling and rushing back like a flooded river breaking through its dikes, and the waters rose halfway up to where the cabin stood on the wide bench.

Jake's first realization of a recovered sense of hearing came with this sound of the chafing flood waters. The contrast between the roar that had deafened him and the gentle lapping of the waves left his ears ringing.

The avalanche had come to rest under its sky-high dust cloud.

Jake ran down the trail and off the bench as far as he could go. Through the thinning dust curtain he saw the width of the gorge piled almost straight up with fresh red earth, skinned tree trunks, and rocks of every size. The avalanche had filled the gorge beyond the narrow defile. Its destructive force had extended to a point even beyond the limit of its wall. Jake had to find a new path between boulders higher than his head, and over logs and slides of shale.

Rocks were still rolling down under the veil of dust. And Jake thought it would be well to retreat to the cabin. Just as he turned back he heard a cry that froze his blood.

Breathless, with heart pounding in his breast, he listened. More than once in his life had he heard the shrill sound made by a horse in extreme terror or injured near to death. This was how Jake interpreted the sound. His heart jumped and he began to breathe again. Then the cry pealed out louder than before.

Jake began frantically climbing in the direction from which he thought the horse's scream had come. The going was rough, over the loose debris flung off by the avalanche. He reached the line of trees and more level ground. It was wet and very slippery. Rain mixed with snow fell around him.

Then suddenly, close at hand, there rose a harsh, fierce shout. It seemed to Jake that he recognized Verde's voice. He bounded through the wet brush and under the dripping trees.

A moment later he burst into a little glade, across which a good-sized pine had fallen. And on the side toward Jake, close to the wet earth, protruded a pair of boots equipped with long bright spurs. Jake recognized them. They did not move. The legs which wore them were pinned to the ground!

Like a panther, Jake leaped over the log. He found himself looking down into the ash-white, agonized face of Verde. The youth still was conscious. His eyes moved and fixed in an expression of disbelief on Jake's face. Then recognition came and he murmured, "Jake."

"My Gawd—Verde!" cried Jake, falling upon his knees to grasp Verde's writhing hands.

"It got me—Jake," whispered Verde. "Last night—my horse fell on me—broke my leg. . . . I crawled—this far—then—the avalanche—"

"I'll get you out, Verde," declared Jake, and laying hold of the prostrate form, he started to pull.

Verde cursed and beat at his rescuer until he ceased his efforts to drag the fallen man from under the tree trunk.

"Don't," whispered Verde, his face white and drawn, wet with big clammy drops of sweat, and jaw quivering. "Don't touch me. . . . I'm done for. . . . But thank Gawd—you've come to—end my misery."

Then Jake awoke to the horror of the facts. Verde lay crushed beneath the pine. It had caught him across the legs almost to his hips. Jake saw a white leg bone protruding through Verde's overalls. The end of the bone was black with dirt.

If there were other bodily injuries, as no doubt there were, Jake could not see them. Verde's arms were free, his chest was apparently sound. But there was a bloody cut on his head.

Again Verde screamed and the unearthly sound broke Jake's nerve and strength. He let go, shaking in every nerve of his body. He had seen another leg bone come protruding out, bloody and white, through Verde's overalls.

"For Gawd's sake, man," panted Verde, "don't let me die by slow torture this way!"

He lay there, transfixing Jake with eyes Jake found almost unendurable to meet.

"Jake—old boy—fer the love of Gawd, put me out—of my misery!"

Jake could only shake his head slowly.

"Shoot me, Jake. . . . I cain't stand it. . . . No use anyhow. . . . I'm smashed. . . . Kill me!"

"Verde!"

"Don't waste time!" pleaded Verde, the blue fire of his eyes momentarily burning away the mist of anguish. "Every second is worse than hellfire! . . . If you have any mercy—kill me!"

"No!"

"But Jake—dear old brother—you don't savvy," went on the pleading husky voice. "I'll bless you—in the hereafter. . . . I beg you. . . . Jake, you saved me once—when we were—young 'uns. You know—down at Lost Boy Ford! You were brother to me then—an' always you've been. . . . But now the great thing is—to spare me—more of this. . . . Cain't you see? Why, old boy, I'd do it—fer you. . . . I swear to Gawd I would. . . . Jake—if you—love me—end my misery!"

Jake's nerveless hand groped for his gun. He seemed numbed. All the sweetness of the years rushed into this one supreme moment—unbearable in its heartshocking agony.

Verde was praying now for deliverance. The deathly radiance of his face seemed to come already from that other world he sought. His face was almost unearthly beautiful then—and it seemed as if the power to command came from beyond life itself. For a moment he almost overcame Jake's resistance. But now a strength almost as great as the avalanche that had caught them seized upon Jake's heart and mind, and the spell was broken.

When Verde saw that he had failed, he snatched at Jake's gun with a wild and tortured cry. Jake flung it far from him.

Then Verde sank back unconscious. And Jake, whipping out his knife, began to dig frantically at the soft earth under Verde's imprisoned legs.

He scooped out a hole on one side, then on the other. Presently he reached under the tree and dug farther. In a few more moments he was able to drag Verde gently from under the log that had imprisoned him.

Then he knelt beside the still form, not daring to look at the white face. He placed a shaking, muddy hand on Verde's breast. Verde's heart still was beating faintly. Realization that his brother still lived made a giant out of Jake.

Sheathing the knife, he lifted the limp form in his arms and strode down to the trail.

The rain had let up a little. The dust was settling. And there came a brightening of the sky, one of the false hopes that such storms hold out in their early stages. As he reached the cabin he noted that the rain was changing to snow.

~7~

VERDE OPENED HIS EYES. HE SMELLED SMOKE AND heard the crackling of a fire. A roof of rough-hewn poles and split shingles slanted above him. He recognized the cabin, and then in a flash he recalled the chain of circumstances that had led to his presence there.

He lay on a couch of boughs in the corner of the cabin. A blanket covered him. Jake was not in the room. Verde felt that the lower parts of his limbs were dead. He had a locked, icy sensation in his breast. He found that he had free use of his hands, and could move his head without difficulty. Jake had removed his boots, one of which had been slit. A bloody ragged leg of his trousers hung over a bench.

The door of the cabin stood open. Verde saw whirling, thin-flaked snow. The ground bore a mantle of white, and the spruce trees looked spectral against the gray gloom. A sound of falling water filled the cabin.

Rapid footfalls struck his ear. The doorway darkened. Jake entered staggering under an enormous armload of fagots. He was wet, and brought in the dank odor of pine. Not until he had deposited the load of wood in a corner next to the huge stone fireplace did he observe that Verde was conscious.

"By glory—you've come to!" he exclaimed, and the haggard darkness of his face brightened in a homely grin.

"Reckon—I have," replied Verde. Speaking was difficult and his voice pitifully weak.

"It took so long," said Jake, with immense relief. "I thought—I was afraid. . . . Verde, are you sufferin'—much?"

"Cain't tell. Feel daid in my legs an' sort of queer here," rejoined Verde, indicating his breast.

"I'm thankful you've no orful pain like this mawnin'."

"What time of day is it?"

"Late afternoon."

"An' I've been unconscious all day long?"

"You shore have."

They looked long into each other's face. Verde's faculties were growing acute. He saw that Jake was laboring under an enormous strain. How strange! Jake was usually so cool, so easy, so sure.

"Jake, old boy, how bad am I hurt?"

"Turrible—bad—all right," replied Jake, swallowing hard.

"Wal, just how and where?"

"There's a cut on your head, clear to the bone. Your right leg is broke below the knee. One bone. I set thet—an' got it in splints. But your—left leg—"

"Got you stumped, hey?" asked Verde as Jake shook his head and gulped.

"Smashed—an' the bones splintered all to hell."

"Ahuh! Must have bled a lot."

"Bled? You shore bled like a stuck pig. But I got thet stopped." .

"Wal, is that all, Jake? Honest Injun now?"

"All I'm sure about. First off there was blood runnin' from your mouth. That scared me. But you haven't bled any more fer hours."

"Ahuh! . . . An' what else are we up against, old boy?"

Jake lifted his hands in a helpless, half-frantic gesture of despair.

"Verde! If the avalanche didn't shut us in forever we're shore snowed up for the winter."

"I was figurin' somethin' like," replied Verde quietly, and closed his eyes. He could not endure to look at Jake any longer just then. Jake was more than appalled by the tragedy. And Verde began to ponder over a meaning for it.

"Verde, you asked me to be honest," went on Jake hesitantly. "An' I'm tellin' you—only a miracle can save us."

Verde noted that Jake used the plural. Perhaps it was only a slip of speech in the seriousness of the moment. Still the implication of a prayer for that one saving miracle was strong. From under his half-closed eyelids Verde watched Jake as he busied himself over the cooking utensils and the fire. Anyone who knew Jake could have told that he was not himself. He was restless, exceedingly nervous, now hurried and again abstracted. He would seem to forget the meal he was preparing and then he would suddenly remember it. He walked aimlessly about the room, took up tasks irrelevant to the hour and left them abruptly, unfinished. He went outdoors and returned for no reason that was evident. Once he came in with an armload of wood, only to carry it out again. And always the only consistent action he seemed to be performing was to turn every little while tragic, deep-set, fearful eyes in the direction of Verde.

At last he managed to get supper ready.

"Verde, can you eat or drink?" he asked.

"I crave cold water. Thet's all. Put some snow in it," replied Verde.

Jake brought it and set it at Verde's elbow.

The afternoon waned and soon night fell. The soft, seeping, sweeping, rustling sound of falling snow almost imperceptibly increased. Around the eaves of the cabin and in the spruces the wind sighed mournfully. From the heights came the faint roar of the storm.

Jake sat in the firelight and Verde watched him. It must have continued so for a long time. Often Jake would replenish the dying fire, which would crackle and flare up and again light up the cabin. It seemed to Verde that Jake was trying not to surrender to a situation that he knew was hopeless. First the natural shock following the desperate accident to Verde, and now the realization of their being shut in, surely lost together. Verde read it all in Jake's dark face.

Jake had meant to kill him. He had wanted him dead! In the humiliation of being whipped before their friends and relatives, and in the jealousy of the hour, and in the subsequent recognition that Kitty Mains loved him no more than she loved Verde, Jake had succumbed to the lust to kill.

When Verde sent word to Jake that he knew where to find him if he wanted satisfaction, Verde had hoped nothing more would come of it. Nothing more except that Kitty should choose one of them! He had hoped, but he had doubted. And here they were, doomed by the avalanche to the same fate. And poor Jake had awakened too late from the horror of his hate for him. It was Jake's fault that they had come to Black Gorge at a season when they should have shunned it. His fault, too, the horror of Verde's crushed legs and the lingering death to come!

In the dark lonely hours of that night, when the flickering firelight played upon Jake's tortured face, Verde learned how awful it must be for Jake. For himself he did not care. Even if he could have been saved he would not have welcomed it. What good of life hobbling about on maimed legs? But for Jake's sake he began to want to live. And as the hours dragged by this desire grew.

Toward morning Jake tiptoed over to peer down at Verde, and then, thinking him asleep, he lay down beside him, very quietly.

But Verde was far from asleep. The pangs of agony had reawakened in his numbed leg. The fire flickered, casting its fantastic shadows on the rude walls of the cabin, flickered, faded, and died. Then blackness reigned. Outside the snow seeped and whirled and, with silky rustle, beat against the cabin. Sometimes vagrant flakes blew through the little window and fell cool and wet upon Verde's face. The wind mourned. Once when it lulled Verde heard the wild, lonely cry of a wolf.

Verde's body seemed weighted by lead. The desperate desire to move had to be yielded to. And the slightest movement of his lower muscles was equivalent to plunging ten thousand red-hot spikes into quivering flesh. But he endured, and fought the strange indifference that stole over his mind.

He must live for Jake's sake. Jake—who had wanted him dead! What a queer thing—that Jake could have imagined that he would be happier with his old friend out of the way!

Dawn broke. Verde was careful to look wide-awake and more cheerful when Jake turned to him.

"How are you, Verde?"

"Rarin' to go—if we only could," replied Verde. "Pile out, Jake, an' when you've had breakfast I want to talk to you."

"Verde! You're not sinkin'?"

"Would you expect me to be soarin'? I haven't sprouted wings yet," returned Verde.

Jake moved about with a synthetic haste that would have been ludicrous if it had not been so pathetic. Every one of his actions proved that he believed his earnestness futile.

"Open the door an' let's look out," said Verde.

Black Gorge was now white, except for the lake which had risen nearly to the edge of the bench.

"Reckon it won't snow heavy down heah," rejoined Jake.

"Is the air cold? I don't 'pear to feel it."

"Nope. It's warm yet, an' that means more snow. But winter shore has set in."

"Wal, Jake, let's talk," replied Verde. "Leave the door open so it'll be light."

Jake drew a bench to Verde's bedside and looked down upon him with the miserable eyes of a dog that knows it has been beaten.

"All right, Verde, I'll listen," he said. But there was not the slightest indication of hope in look or tone.

"What's to be done?" asked Verde brightly.

Jake spread wide his hands with an air of dejection.

"Jake, you've got it figgered this way," went on Verde. "Nobody could get to us, even if they knew where we are. We cain't climb out in the snow. An' I've got to die pronto—an' then you'll starve to death?"

"Not starve, Verde," returned Jake hoarsely. But he had acquiesced with Verde's summary of the situation. He dropped his face in his big broad hands, and tears trickled between his fingers.

"Miracles do happen, Jake," said Verde.

Jake made a sharp gesture of despair.

"Yes. Dad might find us. But even so—he couldn't save you."

"Old boy, is that what matters so much?" asked Verde softly.

"Reckon it's all—that—matters," replied Jake brokenly.

"Well, then, you must be up an' doin'."

"Verde, my mind's stopped workin'."

"Mine hasn't, an' don't you forget it," returned Verde. "Mine's just begun. . . . Jake, you know that my leg as it is—all smashed—will soon mortify. An' it'd kill me pronto."

"Hell, man! You needn't tell me that," Jake replied.

"You've got to cut my leg off," returned Verde slowly and evenly.

"My Gawd, Verde! . . . I—I couldn't," gasped Jake.

"Sure you could. Now think sense, Jake. It's my only chance. You could cut it off—if I told you how—an' if I'd stand it."

Jake was pale and sweating. His big hands opened and shut. His homely, battered face was working.

"Yes, I might. It's this idea that takes my nerve. . . . You—you might die while I was doin' it!"

"Of course I might. That's the chance. But I think I

wouldn't. An' it's damn sure I'll die if you don't. Let's take the chance—my only chance."

"Lord, if I had the nerve!" cried Jake, and he leaped up to pace the room.

"Come back here. . . . Now listen," went on Verde, growing inspired with his plan. "I tell you it's a great idea. An' you can do it!"

"How about the big arteries in your leg?" Jake boomed. "I had one hell of a time stoppin' the bleedin'."

"You mustn't let me bleed any more."

"How about—that splintered bone?"

"You'll saw it off above the break where it's smashed."

"Saw! We haven't anythin' but the big crosscut saw. It'd be impossible to use that."

"There's a three-cornered file we brought to sharpen that saw. You'll make a saw out of your big huntin' knife."

"How?" burst out Jake incredulously.

"File the back of it into sharp saw teeth."

"Reckon I might," muttered Jake doubtfully. Still the idea was sinking in. "But even if I . . . Verde, you forget the worst danger."

"Boy, this is my leg an' my life. You can gamble I'm not forgettin' anythin'!"

"But blood poisonin'! . . . That couldn't be prevented. We've nothin' to—"

"Wrong. We've got fire!" flashed Verde.

Jake stared at him, dominated by Verde's tremendous force.

"Fire?" he echoed.

"Listen. You're sure thick-headed. All we got to do is plan it right—then work fast. My job is to bear it—yours to make it a clean, quick one. . . . You'll sharpen both our huntin' knives. Sharp as razors.

You'll file the back of the long blade into a saw. Then you'll scour a pot an' heat water to boilin'. You'll put the knives in that. Then you'll have your straight brandin' iron in the fire. It must be red hot. Shore you know how slick you are with a brandin' iron? . . . Wal, now. You'll make sure where to cut my leg above the mashed place. You'll bind it tight, so it cain't bleed. Then when all's ready you'll cut the flesh all round, quick an' clean, clear to the bone. Then you'll saw through the bone. Then you'll grab your red-hot brandin' iron an' burn the stub across. That'll sear bone an' arteries an' flesh. You'll loosen the cord, an' wrap my leg in a clean towel or shirt. . . . An' that's all."

"That's all!" blazed Jake. "Good Gawd, Verde! . . . Can you stand it?"

"I can an' will, old boy. I reckon it'll not be as bad as we think. For there's not much feelin' left in that leg."

"When?" gasped Jake. The excitement of the idea had gripped him. The thought that there might still be a chance to save Verde's life was all-consuming.

"Right now!" replied Verde. He had convinced Jake to undertake the terrible responsibility! Convinced him by persuasion, and in the end by falsehood, because during the excitement of this discussion the numbed leg had revived to exquisite pain. But Verde swore in his soul that he would endure and live.

Jake became actuated by supreme, uplifting, galvanizing hope. He was a changed man. Swiftly, quick and hard, he went at the preliminary tasks. He built a roaring fire. He scoured a big iron pot until it shone. He filled it with water and put it on to boil. He scraped all the rust off the branding iron, gave it a polish, and then thrust it in the heart of the red coals. Next he sharpened the knives, and filed the back of the blade of the long one. He was deft and sure, absorbed in each task. It took a long time to notch the blade into a saw and to sharpen the notches, but at last he was satisfied.

"Let me see it, Jake," asked Verde.

It was a ten-inch blade, worn thin from use. Verde felt the sharp teeth.

"Wal, Jake, that'll do the trick pronto," said Verde as coolly as if it was the bone of a horse or steer they were talking about.

"Lucky I've some clean soft shirts," returned Jake. "Ma put them in my bag."

"Good. Tear one up into strips."

"Now what next?" asked Jake, rolling up his sleeves.

"You'll want my leg on somethin' solid. Knock off the top of the bench."

Jake did so, and stripping off the blanket that covered Verde he slipped the board under his shattered leg.

"Verde, ought I to tie you?" asked Jake in solemn earnestness.

"No, Jake, I'll not make a fuss. Don't worry about me. Just you have everythin' ready—then be quick. Make it a clean job. Savvy?"

"I'll have it off quicker'n you can say Jack Robinson," replied Jake.

The boyhood term, used so unconsciously, recalled to Verde the faraway past.

A ponderous blackness seemed to float slowly before Verde's sight. The cabin was dim, vague, like the unreality of a dream.

He lay like a stone, with no power to move, yet his body seemed aquiver in a mighty convulsion of nerves—a million shocks of agony that ranged through him. A tremendous current swelled and burned in his marrow, like a boring worm of fire, up his spine, into his brain.

~8~

IT WAS NIGHT, AND OUTSIDE THE STORM MOANED and wailed and raged. The shadows cast by the fire flickered their last; the red glow of the dying embers faded.

Jake had fallen into the sleep of exhaustion.

But Verde was hovering on the verge of a great and eternal sleep. He knew that death for him was very close. He felt the cool sweet winds of oblivion; he saw the wide, vacant, naked hallway of the beyond, the dim, mystic spiritland; he heard the strange alluring voices. He had only to let go. And every atom of his racked body clamored to be freed. But Verde held on.

It came a thousand times—that wraithlike presence, the specter that contended with Verde's unquenchable will. And then it came no more.

One morning Verde awoke from a deep slumber that had followed his night of agony.

The storm was over. A marble-white and glistening world of snow shone dazzlingly bright from the cabin doorway. Verde heard the sharp ringing of an ax. He saw that one end of the cabin was neatly stacked with firewood. A cheerful blaze crackled on the hearth.

Verde felt a surge of life within him. The crisis was past. The pangs of his poor maimed body were innumerable; but the great rending torture had ebbed and passed away.

Jake entered to greet him with a glad shout.

Another day Verde began to take nourishment that Jake most carefully prepared, and sparingly doled out.

"Shore you're hungry," he agreed, with his eager smile. "But I cain't let you eat much yet. An' for that matter we're both goin' to get good an' damn hungry before the snow melts."

"Reckon I forgot," replied Verde in his weak voice. "How are we fixed for grub?"

"Pretty darn lucky," said Jake fervently. "We always packed up more canned stuff than we ever used. An' there's a lot, some fruit an' milk, but most vegetables. There's a sack of flour an' a couple sacks of beans. Coffee not a great deal, but lots of sugar. There's a hundred pounds of salt that I packed up last spring to cure hides. Lucky that was! An' I've hung up three deer I shot, an' one of my horses. The meat's froze solid. An' I guess that's all."

"Pretty lucky, yes," replied Verde. "But it's a long way from enough. Let's see—what's the date?"

"I don't know exactly. It's well on in November. I'll keep track of days."

"We're snowed up for five months."

"Wal, Verde, it seemed turrible at furst, before I felt shore of you comin' round, but it doesn't faze me now."

"All the same, old boy, it's far the biggest job you ever tackled," replied Verde.

"Reckon so. But don't you worry," said Jake reassuringly. "We'll go easy with our grub. I always was a meat eater, you know, an' I can live on meat. I'll find my other horse an' kill him. Then I saw elk tracks up the canyon, but I didn't want to take time to trail them. I'll do it soon. No, I'm more worried about scarcity of wood than meat. You see there's a couple of feet of snow on, an' down timber is hard to locate."

"The avalanche must have fetched down more wood than we'll need."

"Shore," said Jake, slapping his leg. "I never thought of that. Reckon I sort of shunned the avalanche end of our prison. But with lots of wood I can beat this game."

Verde noted that from this time on Jake was outdoors most of the daylight hours. To be sure, the days were short. But Verde soon became convinced that dry wood and fresh meat were harder to procure than Jake had acknowledged.

Jake ministered to Verde's comfort and health with the care of a mother. Indeed, as days went by he grew more tender in his ministrations; and as Verde's pains lessened and he showed signs of renewing strength, Jake's unspoken worry lessened and he grew happy.

It dawned upon Verde, after a while, that Jake was happier than he had ever been, even before Kitty Mains had come into their lives. Verde guessed at the first flush of this discovery that Jake's happiness came from having saved him, and from the daily service the situation made imperative. But after a while Verde altered this conviction, and arrived at the conclusion that it came from a revival of Jake's earlier love for him. Anyway, Jake's care of him was very sure and very beautiful. Verde never ceased to thank God that he had made the superhuman fight to hold on to life. It had been solely for Jake's sake, but now he began to be glad for his own. He knew that he would manage somehow to ride a horse again.

One night after supper, with the cabin warm and cozy in the firelight and the snow pattering again against the walls, Jake sat a long time staring into the fire. Every once in a while he would throw on a few chips. Finally he turned a changed and softened face to Verde—a face that revealed a beautiful, strange smile and a warm light in his eyes.

"Verde, I reckon it's no exaggeration to say you're out of danger. Your leg has healed. You're on the mend."

"Yes, thanks to you, old boy," returned Verde gratefully.

"Well, you can thank me all you like, but I'm thankin' Gawd. . . . An', Verde, are you forgettin' how you come to be here in this shape?"

"Reckon I am, now you make me think."

Jake paused to moisten his lips, and his big hand smoothed his long hair.

"I hope you can forgive me, Verde."

"There's nothin' to forgive. I'm as much to blame as you. An' mebbe more."

"Wal, we won't argue thet. . . . Do you ever think of Kitty Mains?"

"Shore I do—a lot. When I cain't help myself."

"Verde, you loved Kitty somethin' turrible, didn't you?"

"I'm afraid I did."

"But you do—yet?" demanded Jake intensely, as if any intimation otherwise would be sacrilege.

"All right. Yes, I do yet," replied Verde, hastening to help Jake to his revelation, whatever it was to be.

"Shore, I'm glad. It wouldn't seem fair to Kitty if our—our differences an' this trouble made you love her less. Because, Verde—I know Kitty loved you more than me."

"How do you know that?" asked Verde curiously.

"I reckon I found it out thinkin'. Somethin' came to me lyin' there awake so many nights. An' it was this. Kitty has two natures same as she has eyes. Now I was always easy with girls. Guess I must have a little

of girl nature in me. Anyway my coaxin' an' tender
kind of love must have appealed to Kitty's softer side.
But that side wasn't Kitty's deepest an' strongest.
She's more devil than angel, you can bet. She'd need
to be tamed, an' I never could do it. She'd soon tire of
me. . . . I always saw how Kitty flared up when you
came around. If I'd have been honest with myself I'd
of known what it meant. But I never knew until that
night of the last dance. It nearly killed me then, but
I've lived to be glad. . . . Verde, I reckon mebbe Kitty
isn't all you an' I dreamed she was. But she is what she
is an' we both love her. Now since we've been here
alone I've reasoned it all out. Mebbe Kitty really does
love you best. She ought to, you're so handsome,
Verde. So I'm givin' up my share in her to you."

"But, Jake—" began Verde feebly.

"There's not any buts," interrupted Jake. "I've
settled it. I know I'm right. An' I know this will help
you to get well an' strong quicker 'n anythin' else in
the world."

Verde closed his eyes. He was troubled and shaken,
and yet glad to have any expostulation on his part so
summarily dismissed. But he knew in his heart that he
had not accepted Jake's ultimatum, and that a tremendous issue still loomed in the vague future. Just now he
discovered how weak he was, both physically and
spiritually. It was good to sink down—to realize that
slumber would come. Good old Jake! . . . Verde was a
little boy again, wandering along the road. He came to
a stream where the water ran swiftly and the leaves
floated down. The white sycamore trees stood up like
ghosts. He did not want to go back to the wagon, for
his stepfather hated him and beat him. . . . He was lost
and he began to be afraid. Then a barefooted boy came
out of the brush. "My name's Jake," the boy said.
"What's yours?" And craftily he would not tell because he wished to stay.

~ 9 ~

THE DEAD, COLD WHITE WINTER SHUT DOWN UPON Black Gorge. The short days and the long nights passed. Verde slept most of the time. Jake labored at his tasks. Sometimes after supper he would play checkers with Verde on a rude board of his own construction. Or they held council over the all-important speculations of when and how they would dare attempt to get out of the gorge. Or more often they talked over the nearer and more serious problem of fighting the cold and starvation. They never mentioned Kitty Mains. Jake's peace and serenity had somehow been communicated to Verde.

It was a wonderful occasion for both when Verde rose from his bed and hobbled about the cabin on the crutch Jake had made. From that day Verde's progress grew more rapid. He looked forward to the supreme test that was to come—the climbing out of the canyon. He wanted to be able to help himself again. Jake had become a gaunt bearded giant, hardy as a pine.

It was true that he could thrive on a meat diet. But their meat was dwindling, and if Jake did not soon make a lucky stalk their supply would be exhausted and they must face starvation. Every day Jake hunted in the recesses of the winding gorge. Several times he had been on the eve of sighting elk, but the advent of night and fresh snow covering the tracks each time had frustrated his hopes.

The days passed, and the hours of sunlight lengthened. The snow melted from the cabin roof and then disappeared from the south slope of the gorge. The icy clutch of winter loosened. Sometimes a warm, balmy breath of wind came wandering through the depths of the gorge.

With spring close at hand they came to the last pound of meat and the last hard biscuit each. Jake, giant that he was, had lately grown much gaunter. He had been sacrificing his food for Verde. When Verde discovered this he refused to eat at all unless Jake had an equal share. So they cooked the last pound of frozen meat.

Then Jake left with his rifle. Verde could now manage very well with his crutch. He did the chores while Jake hunted. There was a beautiful sky that afternoon. Verde gazed up wistfully over the pink-tinged snow ridges. Spring was coming. What a winter Jake and he had put in! Yet Verde would not have wanted it different, even to the recovery of his leg. Jake's labors had been as great as his own sufferings. Together they had conquered something more fearful than death. Together they had climbed heights more beautiful than life itself.

Before the sunset flush had paled on the high ridges Jake came staggering in under a load of meat. With a heavy crash he threw down a haunch of elk. He was covered with snow and blood. A pungent animal odor and the scent of the woods emanated from him to fill the cabin.

"Killed a bull an' a yearlin'," he boomed, with his deep-set eyes beaming gladly upon Verde. "They've been hidin' from me all winter. But I found them. . . . An' Verde, soon I'll be makin' a sled to haul you home."

"Say, you great big ragamuffin!" yelled Verde with a joy that matched Jake's own. "I'll walk home on one leg!"

Jake had the impetuosity to make the start soon, but Verde had the wisdom and courage to wait awhile longer. The fresh meat would build up their strength and the longer they delayed the less snow they would have to combat.

During these last days Jake cut a zigzag trail in the snow up the side of the avalanche. This side, being on the north, did not get the sun except for a brief while each day. The obstacle that imprisoned them, however, was the deep snow on top. Jake climbed high enough to see that the south slopes everywhere showed great patches of black where it had thawed. He was jubilant.

"Verde, I'm rarin' to go. Once on top the rest will be easy!"

The night before the day they meant to undertake the climb upon which so much depended, Verde came out with something that had for long obsessed his mind, and had been greatly contributary to the source of his own tranquillity.

"Wal, Jake, now it's time to get somethin' off my own chest," he said, with all the calmness he could muster.

"Ahuh?" asked Jake rather sharply. Evidently he did not like Verde's look.

"I didn't say so before, but I never agreed with you on that deal about Kitty Mains."

"No! . . . Say, ain't it kinda late in the day to—"

"Late, but better than never. . . . Jake, old boy, I cain't accept what you wanted. I never agreed with you. An' I simply won't let you give up Kitty for me."

Jake turned red under his matted beard. He left off the task in hand and stood up to confront Verde.

"Don't you love Kitty same as I do?" he demanded.

Verde had his argument all planned, and the fact that

in some degree it departed from strict veracity caused him no concern.

"Wal, I reckon I did once, but hardly now. This winter has knocked a lot out of me. Then I'm a cripple now, an' I never saw thet women cared a heap for cripples, except with a sort of pity. I cain't work as I used to, an' I'll be dependent upon your pa. . . . Jake, he's been a dad to me, same as you've been a brother, Gawd bless you! But after all my name's not Dunton. I haven't any real name to give a woman. . . . Now all these things helped me to make up my mind. Fust an' last though, the biggest reason is that no matter what you say against it, I believe Kitty loves you best."

"Verde, you're a doggone liar!" declared Jake huskily.

"Well, if she didn't last fall, it's a shore bet she will now. I'm only half a man, Jake. . . . So let's shake hands on it."

"What if I won't?"

"I'd hate to say, Jake. Fact is, I don't know. Because my thinkin' didn't get so far. I might never leave this cabin with you. . . . See it my way, Jake. You got to! We've come through hell, an' we're happy in spite of it—perhaps because of it. I don't know. Only I'd never be happy again if you won't take it my way."

Jake wrung Verde's hand, and turned away, mute and shaken, his head bowed.

Next morning at sunrise they started. Verde had only his crutch. Jake had a blanket strapped to his back, and he carried some strips of cooked meat in his pocket and a rope in his hand. He had carried the sled high up on the slope to use in case the snow was not gone from the ridge top and the south slope beyond.

The plan was to climb very slowly, foot by foot, to husband Verde's strength. Two things became manifest during the early hours of the ascent—first, that the difficulties were greater than they had anticipated, and secondly that Verde had amazing strength and endurance.

But he gave out before they reached the top. Whereupon Jake took Verde over his shoulder, and carried him as he would a sack of meal. All winter Jake had packed heavy logs down to the cabin—packed them when he might have cut them into lesser lengths. But he had looked far ahead—to this terrible ascent out of Black Gorge. He was indeed a giant. Verde marveled at him. On the other hand, he was as slow and cautious as he was powerful and enduring. He carried Verde for only short distances, sometimes only a few yards. Then he would lower him to his foot and crutch on some high place. Thus, when he had caught his breath again, he would not have to bend down and lift Verde.

Up and up he toiled. The real Herculean labor began at the end of the trail Jake had cut in the snow. Verde almost despaired. But he could not flinch in the face of this magnificent and invincible courage. Jake had meant to kill him once and now he meant to save him. It was written. Verde felt it. And when his reason argued that Jake must soon fall broken and spent something told him no physical obstacle could conquer this man.

The afternoon waned. Sunset found them in deep snow. But before night came Jake had dragged Verde over the top of the ridge and down onto bare ground. There he fell, gasping and voiceless.

Verde set about gathering dead brush, which he piled in the lee of a large rock. Jake came presently, and helped him build a roaring fire. Then they heated the strips of meat and ate them. Jake cut spruce boughs and made a bed of them between the fire and the rock. Verde lay warm under the blanket, but he could not go to sleep immediately. Jake hunched close to the fire. His heart was too full for words, or sleep, or anything but a silent realization of deliverance and happiness.

The night wind moaned, but not with the moan of winter.

Sunrise found them on their way down the vast slope of brown and green which was dotted with patches of snow. The descent was easy, though slow. They had only to thread their way between the un-thawed drifts and the thickets of brush. For a load-stone of hope they had their first sight of the Dunton ranch, a tiny green grass plot far in the distance, but coming ever closer.

Again sunset burned red and gold in the sky. Verde could now gaze back and up at the rim, bold and beautiful with its belt of bright-colored cliffs and its fringed line of black pines.

With Jake's arm upholding Verde, they staggered across the ranch field, to encounter Dunton coming out of the cabin. He dropped a bucket he had been carrying.

"Jane—wife—come quick!" he yelled.

Jake waved a tired hand.

"Dad, it's me an' Verde!"

"My Gawd! You infernal scarecrows!"

Then the mother came, white-faced, to scream a wonderful, ecstatic welcome.

The warm, bright living room seemed like heaven to Verde. He could only look and feel, as he lay back, propped in a comfortable rocking chair. How good to be home! That wild, white mantled gorge retreated from his memory.

It was Jake who talked, who laughed when his mother wept.

Dunton cast eyes both happy and sad over his returned sons.

"So thet's your story," he said. "Wal, the Tonto

never heard its beat. I reckon I'm proud of you both.
. . . But, my Gawd, boys, the pity of it! . . . All fer
nothin'! All for a slip of a pop-eyed girl who wasn't
worth your little finger, let alone a leg! Shore! Folks
hadn't even stopped talkin' about your fight when she
up an' married young Stillwell."

from missouri

~1~

WITH JINGLING SPURS A TALL COWBOY STALKED OUT of the post office to confront his three comrades who were just then crossing the wide street from the saloon opposite.

"Look heah," he said, shoving a letter under their noses. "Which one of you longhorns has wrote her again?"

From a gay, careless trio his listeners suddenly looked blank, then intensely curious. They stared at the handwriting on the letter.

"Tex, I'm a son-of-a-gun if it ain't from Missouri!" exclaimed Andy Smith, his lean red face bursting into a smile.

"It shore is," declared Nevada.

"From Missouri!" echoed Panhandle Ames.

"Wal?" asked Tex, almost with a snort.

The three cowboys drew back to look from Tex to one another, and then back at Tex.

"It's from *her*," went on Tex, his voice hushing on the pronoun. "You all know thet handwritin'. Now how about this deal? We swore none of us would write agin to this heah schoolmarm. But some one of you has double-crossed the outfit."

Loud and simultaneous protestations of innocence

arose from his comrades. But it was evident that Tex did not trust them, and that they did not trust him or each other.

"Say, boys," said Panhandle suddenly. "I see Beady in there lookin' darn sharp at us. Let's get off in the woods somewhere."

"Back to the bar," replied Nevada. "I reckon we'll all need bracers."

"Beady!" exclaimed Tex as they turned across the street. "He could be to blame as much as any of us."

"Shore. It'd be more like Beady," replied Nevada. "But Tex, your mind ain't workin'. Our lady friend from Missouri has wrote before without gettin' any letter from us."

"How do we know thet?" demanded Tex suspiciously. "Shore the boss's typewriter is a puzzle, but it could hide tracks. Savvy, pards?"

"Doggone it, Tex, you need a drink," returned Panhandle peevishly.

They entered the saloon and strode up to the bar, where from all appearances Tex was not the only one to seek artificial strength. Then they repaired to a corner, where they took seats and stared at the letter Tex threw down before them.

"From Missouri, all right," averred Panhandle, studying the postmark. "Kansas City, Missouri."

"It's her writin'," added Nevada, in awe. "Shore I'd know thet out of a million letters."

"Ain't you goin' to read it to us?" asked Andy Smith.

"Mr. Frank Owens," replied Tex, reading from the address on the letter. "Springer's Ranch. Beacon, Arizona. . . . Boys, this heah Frank Owens is all of us."

"Huh! Mebbe he's a darn sight more," added Andy.

"Looks like a lowdown trick we're to blame for," resumed Tex, seriously shaking his hawklike head.

"Heah we reads in a Kansas City paper about a schoolteacher wantin' a job out in dry Arizony. An' we ups an' writes her an' gets her ararin' to come. Then when she writes and tells us she's *not over forty*—then we quits like yellow coyotes. An' we four anyhow shook hands on never writin' her agin. Wal, somebody did, an' I reckon you all think me as big a liar as I think you are. But thet ain't the point. Heah's another letter to Mr. Owens an' I'll bet my saddle it means trouble. Shore I'm plumb afraid to read it."

"Say, give it to me," demanded Andy. "I ain't afraid of any woman."

Tex snatched the letter out of Andy's hand.

"Cowboy, you're too poor educated to read letters from ladies," observed Tex. "Gimme a knife, somebody. . . . Say, it's all perfumed."

Tex impressively spread out the letter and read laboriously:

> *Kansas City, Mo.*
> *June 15*

Dear Mr. Owens:

> *Your last letter has explained away much that was vague and perplexing in your other letters.*
> *It has inspired me with hope and anticipation. I shall not take time now to express my thanks, but hasten to get ready to go west. I shall leave tomorrow and arrive at Beacon on June 19, at 4:30 P.M. You see I have studied the timetable.*

> *Yours very truly,*
> JANE STACEY

Profound silence followed Tex's perusal of the letter. The cowboys were struck completely dumb. Then suddenly Nevada exploded:

"My Gawd, fellers, today's the nineteenth!"

"Wal, Springer needs a schoolmarm at the ranch," finally spoke up the more practical Andy. "There's half a dozen kids growin' up without no schoolin', not to talk about other ranches. I heard the boss say so hisself."

"Who the hell did it?" demanded Tex, in a rage with himself and his three accomplices.

"What's the sense in hollerin' about thet now?" returned Nevada. "It's done. She's comin'. She'll be on the Limited. Reckon we've got five hours. It ain't enough. What'll we *do?*"

"I can get orful drunk in thct time," contributed Panhandle nonchalantly.

"Ahuh! An' leave it all to us," retorted Tex scornfully. "But we got to stand pat on this heah deal. Don't you know this is Saturday an' thet Springer will be in town?"

"Aw, Lord! We're all goin' to get ourselves fired," declared Panhandle. "Serves us right for listenin' to you, Tex. We can all gamble this trick was hatched in your haid."

"Not my haid more'n yours or anybody's," returned Tex hotly.

"Say, you locoed cowpunchers," interposed Nevada. "Quit arguin'. What'll we do?"

"Shore is bad," sighed Andy. "What'll we do?"

"We'll have to tell Springer."

"But, Tex, the boss'd never believe us about not followin' the letters up. He'll fire the whole cussed outfit."

"But he'll have to be told somethin'," returned Panhandle stoutly.

"Shore he will," went on Tex. "I've an idea. It's too late now to turn this poor schoolmarm back. An' somebody'll have to meet her. Somebody's got to borrow a buckboard an' drive her out to the ranch."

"Excuse me!" replied Andy. And Panhandle and Nevada echoed his sentiments.

"I'll ride over on my hoss, an' see you all meet the lady," added Andy.

Tex by now had lost his scowl, but he still did not look as if he favorably regarded Andy's idea.

"Hang it all!" he burst out hotly. "Cain't some of you gents look at it from her side of the fence. Nice fix fer any woman, I say. Somebody ought to get it good fer this mess. If I ever find out—"

"Go on with your grand idea," interposed Nevada.

"You all come with me. I'll get a buckboard. I'll meet the lady an' do the talkin'. I'll let her down easy. An' if I cain't haid her back to Missouri we'll fetch her out to the ranch an' then leave it up to Springer. Only we won't tell her or him or anybody who's the real Frank Owens."

"Tex, that ain't so plumb bad," declared Andy admiringly.

"What *I* want to know is who's goin' to do the talkin' to the boss?" asked Panhandle. "It mightn't be so hard to explain now. But after drivin' up to the ranch with a woman! You all know Springer's shy. Young an' rich, like he is, an' a bachelor—he's been fussed over so he's plumb afraid of girls. An' here you're fetchin' a middle-aged schoolmarm who's romantic an' mushy!—My Gawd! . . . I say, send her home on the next train."

"Pan, you're wise as far as hosses an' cattle goes, but you don't know human nature, an' you're daid wrong about the boss," rejoined Tex. "We're in a bad fix, I'll admit. But I lean more to fetchin' the lady up than sendin' her back. Somebody down Beacon way would get wise. Mebbe the schoolmarm might talk. She'd shore have cause. An' suppose Springer hears about it—that some of us or all of us has played a lowdown trick on a woman. He'd be madder at thet than if we fetched her up. Likely he'll try to make amends. The boss may be shy on girls but he's the squarest man in Arizony. My idea is we'll deny any of us is Frank Owens, an' we'll meet Miss—Miss—what was thet there name?—Miss Jane Stacey and fetch her up to the ranch, an' let *her* do the talkin' to Springer."

During the next several hours, while Tex searched the town for a buckboard and team he could borrow, the other cowboys wandered from the saloon to the post office and back again, and then to the store, the restaurant and back again. The town had gradually filled up with Saturday visitors.

"Boys, there's the boss," suddenly broke out Andy, pointing; and he ducked into the nearest doorway, which happened to be that of another saloon. It was half-full of cowboys, ranchers, Mexicans, tobacco smoke, and noise.

Andy's companions had rushed pell-mell after him; and not until they all got inside did they realize that this saloon was a rendezvous for cowboys decidedly not on friendly terms with Springer's outfit. Nevada was the only one of the trio who took the situation nonchalantly.

"Wal, we're in, an' what the hell do we care for Beady Jones, an' his outfit?" remarked Nevada, plenty loud enough to be heard by others besides his friends.

Naturally they lined up at the bar, and this was not a good thing for young men who had an important engagement ahead of them and who must therefore preserve sobriety. After several rounds of drinks they began to whisper and snicker over the possibility of Tex meeting the boss.

"If only it don't come off until Tex gets our forty-year-old schoolmarm from Missouri with him in the buckboard!" exclaimed Panhandle, in huge glee.

"Shore. Tex, the handsome galoot, is most to blame for this mess," added Nevada. "Thet cowboy won't be above makin' love to Jane, if he thinks we're not around. But, fellers, we want to be there."

"Wouldn't miss seein' the boss meet Tex for a million!" said Andy.

Presently a tall striking-looking cowboy, with dark face and small bright eyes like black beads, detached himself from a group of noisy companions, and confronted the trio, more particularly Nevada.

"Howdy, men," he greeted them, "what you all doin' in here?"

He was coolly impertinent, and his action and query noticeably silenced those in the room. Andy and Panhandle leaned back against the bar. They had been in such situations before and knew who would do the talking for them.

"Howdy, Jones," replied Nevada coolly and carelessly. "We happened to bust in here by accident. Reckon we're usually more p'rtic'lar what kind of company we mix with."

"Ahuh! Springer's outfit is shore a stuck-up lot," sneered Jones, in a loud tone. "So stuck-up they won't even ride around folks' drift fences."

Nevada slightly changed his position.

"Beady, I've had a couple of drinks an' ain't very clearhaided," drawled Nevada. "Would you mind talkin' so I can understand you?"

"Bah! You savvy all right," declared Jones sarcastically. "I'm tellin' you straight what I've been layin' to tell your yallerhaided Texas pard."

"Now you're speakin' English, Beady. Tex an' me are pards, shore. An' I'll take it kind of you to get this talk out of your system. You seem to be chock full of somethin'."

"You bet I'm full an' I'm agoin' to bust," shouted Jones, whose temper evidently could not abide the slow cool speech with which he had been answered.

"Wal, before you bust, explain jist what you mean by Springer's outfit not ridin' around drift fences."

"Easy. You just cut through wire fences," retorted Jones.

"Beady, I hate to call you a lowdown liar, but thet's what you are."

"You're another," yelled Jones. "I seen your Texas Jack cut our drift fence."

Nevada struck out with remarkable swiftness and force. He knocked Jones over upon a card table, with which he crashed to the floor. Jones was so stunned that he did not recover before some of his comrades rushed to him, and helped him to his feet. Then, purple in the face with rage and cursing savagely he jerked for his gun. He got it out, but before he could level it two of his friends seized him and wrestled with him, talking in earnest alarm. But Jones fought them.

"You damn fool," finally yelled one of them. "He's not packin' a gun. It'd be murder."

That brought Jones to his senses, though certainly not to a state of calmness.

"Mr. Nevada—next time you hit town you'd better come heeled," he snarled between his teeth.

"Shore. An thet'll be bad luck for you, Beady," replied Nevada curtly.

Panhandle and Andy drew Nevada out to the street, where they burst into exclamations of mingled excitement and anger. Their swift strides gravitated once more toward the saloon across from the post office.

When they emerged sometime later they were arm in arm, and far from steady on their feet. They paraded up the one main street of Beacon, not in the least conspicuous on a Saturday afternoon. As they were neither hilarious nor dangerous, nobody paid any particular attention to them. Springer, their boss, met them, gazed at them casually, and passed by without sign of recognition. If he had studied the boys closely he might have received an impression that they were clinging to a secret, as well as to each other.

In due time the trio presented themselves at the railroad station. Tex was there, nervously striding up and down the platform, now and then looking at his watch. The afternoon train was nearly due. At the hitching rail below the platform stood a new buckboard and a rather spirited team of horses.

The boys, coming across the wide square, encountered this evidence of Tex's extremity, and struck a posture before it.

"Livery shable outfit, my gosh," said Andy.

"Shon of a gun if it ain't," added Panhandle with a huge grin.

"Thish here Tex shpendin' his money royal," agreed Nevada.

Then Tex saw them. He stared. Suddenly he jumped straight up. Striding to the edge of the platform, with face as red as a beet, he began to curse them.

"Whash masher, ole pard?" asked Andy, who appeared a little less stable than his two comrades.

Tex's reply was another volley of expressive profanity. And he ended with: "—you all yellow quitters to get drunk an' leave me in the lurch. But you gotta get away from heah. I shore won't have you about when thet train comes in."

"Tex, your boss is in town lookin' for you," said Nevada.

"I don't care a damn," replied Tex, with fire in his eye.

"Wait till he shees you," gurgled Andy.

"Tex, he jist ambled past us like we wasn't gennelmen," added Panhandle. "Never sheen us atall."

"No wonder, you drunken cowpunchers," declared Tex in disgust. "Now, I tell you to clear out of heah."

"But, pard, we jist want shee you meet our Jane from Missouri," replied Andy.

"If you all ain't a lot of four-flushers I'll eat my chaps!" burst out Tex hotly.

Just then a shrill whistle announced the arrival of the train.

"You can sneak off now," he went on, "an' leave me to face the music. I always knew I was the only gentleman in Springer's outfit."

The three cowboys did not act upon Tex's sarcastic suggestion, but they hung back, looking at once excited and sheepish and hugely delighted.

The long gray dusty train pulled into the station and stopped with a complaining of brakes. There was only one passenger for Springer—a woman—and she alighted from the coach near where the cowboys stood waiting. She wore a long linen coat and a brown veil that completely hid her face. She was not tall and she was much too slight for the heavy valise the porter handed down to her.

Tex strode swaggeringly toward her.

"Miss—Miss Stacey, ma'am?" he asked, removing his sombrero.

"Yes," she replied. "Are you Mr. Owens?"

Evidently the voice was not what Tex had expected and it disconcerted him.

"No, ma'am, I—I'm not Mister Owens," he said. "Please let me take your bag. . . . I'm Tex Dillon, one of Springer's cowboys. An' I've come to meet you—an' fetch you out to the ranch."

"Thank you, but I—I expected to be met by Mr. Owens," she replied.

"Ma'am, there's been a mistake—I've got to tell you—there ain't any Mister Owens," blurted out Tex manfully.

"Oh!" she said, with a little start.

"You see, it was this way," went on the confused

190

cowboy. "One of Springer's cowboys—not *me*—wrote them letters to you, signin' his name Owens. There ain't no such named cowboy in this whole county. Your last letter—an' here it is—fell into my hands—all by accident, ma'am, it shore was. I took my three friends heah—I took them into my confidence. An' we all came down to meet you."

She moved her head and evidently looked at the strange trio of cowboys Tex had pointed out as his friends. They shuffled forward, but not too eagerly, and they still held on to each other. Their condition, not to consider their state of excitement, could not have been lost even upon a tenderfoot from Missouri.

"Please return my—my letter," she said, turning again to Tex, and she put out a small gloved hand to take it from him. "Then—there is no Mr. Frank Owens?"

"No ma'am, there shore ain't," replied Tex miserably.

"Is there—no—no truth in his—is there no schoolteacher wanted here?" she faltered.

"I think so, ma'am," he replied. "Springer said he needed one. Thet's what started us answerin' the advertisement an' the letters to you. You can see the boss an'—an' explain. I'm shore it will be all right. He's one swell feller. He won't stand for no joke on a poor old schoolmarm."

In his bewilderment Tex had spoken his thoughts, and his last slip made him look more miserable than ever, and made the boys appear ready to burst.

"Poor old schoolmarm!" echoed Miss Stacey. "Perhaps the deceit has not been wholly on one side."

Whereupon she swept aside the enveloping veil to reveal a pale yet extremely pretty face. She was young. She had clear gray eyes and a sweet sensitive mouth. Little curls of chestnut hair straggled down from under her veil. And she had tiny freckles.

Tex stared at this lovely apparition.

"But you—you—the letter says she wasn't over forty," he exclaimed.

"She's not," rejoined Miss Stacey curtly.

Then there were visible and remarkable indications of transformation in the attitude of the cowboy. But the approach of a stranger suddenly seemed to paralyze him. The newcomer was very tall. He strolled up to them. He was booted and spurred. He halted before the group and looked expectantly from the boys to the strange young woman and back again. But for the moment the four cowboys appeared dumb.

"Are—are you Mr. Springer?" asked Miss Stacey.

"Yes," he replied, and he took off his sombrero. He had a deeply tanned frank face and keen blue eyes.

"I am Jane Stacey," she explained hurriedly. "I'm a schoolteacher. I answered an advertisement. And I've come from Missouri because of letters I received from a Mr. Frank Owens, of Springer's Ranch. This young man met me. He has not been very—explicit. I gather that there is no Mr. Owens—that I'm the victim of a cowboy joke. . . . But he said that Mr. Springer wouldn't stand for a joke on a poor old schoolmarm."

"I sure am glad to meet you, Miss Stacey," responded the rancher, with an easy Western courtesy that must have been comforting to her. "Please let me see the letters."

She opened a handbag, and searching in it, presently held out several letters. Springer never even glanced at his stricken cowboys. He took the letters.

"No, not that one," said Miss Stacey, blushing scarlet. "That's one I wrote to Mr. Owens, but didn't mail. It's—hardly necessary to read that."

While Springer read the others she looked at him. Presently he asked for the letter she had taken back. Miss Stacey hesitated, then refused. He looked cool, serious, businesslike. Then his keen eyes swept over the four ill-at-ease cowboys.

"Tex, are you Mister Frank Owens?" he asked sharply.

"I—shore—ain't," gasped Tex.

Springer asked each of the other boys the same question and received decidedly maudlin but negative answers. Then he turned again to the girl.

"Miss Stacey, I regret to say that you are indeed the victim of a lowdown cowboy trick," he said. "I'd apologize for such heathen if I knew how. All I can say is I'm sorry."

"Then—then there isn't any school to teach—any place for me—out here?" she asked, and there were tears in her eyes.

"That's another matter," he replied, with a pleasant smile. "Of course there's a place for you. I've wanted a schoolteacher for a long time. Some of the men out at the ranch have kids an' they sure need a teacher badly."

"Oh, I'm—so glad," she murmured, in evident relief. "I was afraid I'd have to go—all the way back. You see I'm not so strong as I used to be—and my doctor advised a change of climate—dry Western air."

"You don't look sick," he said, with his keen eyes on her. "You look very well to me."

"Oh, indeed, but I'm not very strong," she returned quickly. "But I must confess I wasn't altogether truthful about my age."

"I was wondering about that," he said, gravely. There seemed just a glint of a twinkle in his eye. "Not over forty."

Again she blushed and this time with confusion.

"It wasn't altogether a lie. I was afraid to mention that I was only—young. And I wanted to get the position so much. . . . I'm a good—a competent teacher, unless the scholars are too grown-up."

"The scholars you'll have at my ranch are children," he replied. "Well, we'd better be starting if we are to get there before dark. It's a long ride. Is this all your baggage?"

Springer led her over to the buckboard and helped her in, then stowed the valise under the back seat.

"Here, let me put this robe over you," he said. "It'll be dusty. And when we get up on the ridge it's cold."

At this juncture Tex came to life and he started forward. But Andy and Nevada and Panhandle stood motionless staring at the lovely and now flushed face of the young schoolteacher. Tex untied the halter of the spirited team and they began to prance. He gathered up the reins as if about to mount the buckboard.

"I've got all the supplies an' the mail, Mr. Springer," he said cheerfully, "an' I can be startin' at once."

"I'll drive Miss Stacey," replied Springer dryly.

Tex looked blank for a moment. Then Miss Stacey's clear gray eyes seemed to embarrass him. A tinge of red came into his tanned cheek.

"Tex, you can ride my horse home," said the rancher.

"Thet wild stallion of yours!" exclaimed the cowboy. "Now, Mr. Springer, I shore am afraid of that hoss."

This from the best horseman on the whole range!

Apparently the rancher chose to take Tex seriously.

"He sure is wild, Tex, and I know you're a poor hand with a horse. If he throws you, why you'll still have your own horse."

Miss Stacey turned away her eyes. There was a hint of a smile on her lips. Springer got in beside her, and taking the reins, without another glance at his discomfited cowboys, he spoke to the team and drove away.

~2~

A FEW WEEKS ALTERED MANY THINGS AT SPRINGER'S
Ranch. There was a marvelous change in the dress and
deportment of the cowboys when off duty. There were
some clean and happy and interested children. There
was a rather taciturn and lonely young rancher who
was given to thoughtful dreams and whose keen blue
eyes kept watch on the little adobe schoolhouse
under the cottonwoods. And in Jane Stacey's face
a rich bloom and tan had begun to drive out the city
pallor.

It was not often that Jane left the schoolhouse
without meeting one of Springer's cowboys. She met
Tex most frequently, and according to Andy, that
fact was because Tex was foreman and could send the
boys off to the ends of the range when he had the
notion.

One afternoon Jane encountered the foreman. He
was clean-shaven, bright and eager, a superb figure of
a man. Tex had been lucky enough to have a gun with
him one day when a rattlesnake had frightened the
schoolteacher and he had shot the reptile. Miss Stacey
had leaned against him in her fright; she had been
grateful; she had admired his wonderful skill with a
gun and had murmured that a woman always would be
safe with such a man. Thereafter Tex packed his gun
unmindful of the ridicule of his rivals.

"Miss Stacey, come for a little ride, won't you?" he
asked eagerly.

The cowboys had already taught her how to handle a

horse and to ride; and if all they said of her appearance and accomplishment were true she was indeed worth watching.

"I'm sorry," replied Jane. "I promised Nevada I'd ride with him today."

"I reckon Nevada is miles an' miles up the valley by now," replied Tex. "He won't be back till long after dark."

"But he made an engagement with me," protested the schoolmistress.

"An' shore he has to work. He's ridin' for Springer, an' I'm foreman of this ranch," said Tex.

"You sent him off on some long chase," averred Jane severely. "Now didn't you?"

"I shore did. He comes crowin' down to the bunk-house—about how he's goin' to ride with you an' how we all are not in the runnin'."

"Oh! he did—And what did you say?"

"I says, 'Nevada, I reckon there's a steer mired in the sand up in Cedar Wash. You ride up there an' pull him out.' "

"And then what did he say?" inquired Jane curiously.

"Why, Miss Stacey, shore I hate to tell you. I didn't think he was so—so bad. He jist used the most awful language as was ever heard on this heah ranch. Then he rode off."

"But *was* there a steer mired up in the wash?"

"I reckon so," replied Tex, rather shamefacedly. "Most always is one."

Jane let scornful eyes rest upon the foreman.

"That was a mean trick," she said.

"There's been worse done to me by him, an' all of them. An' all's fair in love an' war. . . . Will you ride with me?"

"No."

"Why not?"

"Because I think I'll ride off alone up Cedar Wash and help Nevada find that mired steer."

"Miss Stacey, you're shore not goin' to ride off alone. Savvy that?"

"Who'll keep me from it?" demanded Jane with spirit.

"I will. Or any of the boys, for thet matter. Springer's orders."

Jane started with surprise and then blushed rosy red. Tex, also, appeared confused at his disclosure.

"Miss Stacey, I oughtn't have said that. It slipped out. The boss said we needn't tell you, but you were to be watched an' taken care of. It's a wild range. You could get lost or thrown from a hoss."

"Mr. Springer is very kind and thoughtful," murmured Jane.

"The fact is, this heah ranch is a different place since you came," went on Tex as if suddenly emboldened. "An' this beatin' around the bush doesn't suit me. All the boys have lost their haids over you."

"Indeed? How flattering!" replied Jane, with just a hint of mockery. She was fond of all her admirers, but there were four of them she had not yet forgiven.

The tall foreman was not without spirit.

"It's true all right, as you'll find out pretty quick," he replied. "If you had any eyes you'd see that cattle raisin' on this heah ranch is about to halt till somethin' is decided. Why, even Springer himself is sweet on you!"

"How dare you!" flashed Jane, blushing furiously.

"I ain't afraid to tell the truth," declared Tex stoutly. "He is. The boys all say so. He's grouchier than ever. He's jealous. Lord! he's jealous! He watches you—"

"Suppose I told him you had dared to say such things?" interrupted Jane, trembling on the verge of a strange emotion.

"Why, he'd be tickled to death. He hasn't got nerve enough to tell you himself."

Jane shook her head, but her face was still flushed. This cowboy, like all his comrades, was hopeless. She was about to attempt to change the topic of the conversation when Tex suddenly took her into his arms. She struggled—and fought with all her might. But he succeeded in kissing her cheek and then the tip of her ear. Finally she broke away from him.

"Now—" she panted. "You've done it—you've insulted me! Now I'll never ride with you again—never even speak to you."

"Shore I didn't insult you," replied Tex. "Jane—won't you marry me?"

"No."

"Won't you be my sweetheart—till you care enough to—to—"

"No."

"But, Jane, you'll forgive me, an' be good friends with me agin?"

"Never!"

Jane did not mean all she said. She had come to understand these men of the range—their loneliness—their hunger for love. But in spite of her sympathy and affection she needed sometimes to appear cold and severe with them.

"Jane, you owe me a good deal—more than you got any idea of," said Tex seriously.

"How so?"

"Didn't you ever guess about me?"

"My wildest flight at guessing would never make anything of you, Texas Jack."

"You'd never have been heah but fer me," he said solemnly.

Jane could only stare at him.

"I meant to tell you long ago. But I shore didn't

have the nerve. Jane I—I was thet there letter-writin' feller. I wrote them letters you got. I am Frank Owens."

"No!" exclaimed Jane. She was startled. That matter of Frank Owens had never been cleared up to her satisfaction. It had ceased to rankle within her breast, but it had never been completely forgotten. She looked up earnestly into the big fellow's face. It was like a mask. But she saw through it. He was lying. He was brazen. Almost, she thought, she saw a laugh deep in his eyes.

"I shore am thet lucky man who found you a job when you was sick an' needed a change. . . . An' thet you've grown so pretty an' so well you owe all to me."

"Tex, if you really were Frank Owens, *that* would make a great difference; indeed I do owe him everything. I would—but I don't believe you are he."

"It's a shore honest Gospel fact," declared Tex. "I hope to die if it ain't!"

Jane shook her head sadly at his monstrous prevarication.

"I don't believe you," she said, and left him standing there.

It might have been mere coincidence that during the next few days both Nevada and Panhandle waylaid the pretty schoolteacher and conveyed to her intelligence by divers and pathetic arguments the astounding fact that each was none other than Mr. Frank Owens. More likely, however, was it attributable to the unerring instinct of lovers who had sensed the importance and significance of this mysterious correspondent's part in bringing health and happiness into Jane Stacey's life. She listened to them with both anger and amusement at their deceit, and she had the same answer for both, "I don't believe you."

Because of these clumsy machinations of the cowboys, Jane had begun to entertain some vague, sweet, and disturbing suspicions of her own as to the real identity of that mysterious cowboy, Frank Owens.

Andy had originality as well as daring. He would have completely deceived Jane if she had not happened, by the merest accident, to discover the relation between him and certain love letters she had begun to find in her desk. She was deceived at first, for the typewriting of the missives was precisely the same as that used in the letters by Frank Owens. Jane surprised herself by the emotion that swept over her as she read the first of the notes. That had given place to a frank realization of the precarious condition of her own heart. When she happened to discover in Andy the writer of these romantic epistles, her dream was shattered. Andy certainly would not carry love letters to her that he did not write. He had merely learned to use the same typewriter, and at opportune times he had slipped the letters into her desk. Jane now began to have her own little romantic secret which she did not even try to put out of her mind. Every letter from the productive "Frank Owens" was disturbing even though she suspected the source. Therefore she decided to put a check to Andy's off-duty avocation. She addressed a note to him and wrote, "Dear Andy. Do you remember that day at the train when you thought I was a poor old schoolmarm you swore that you were not Frank Owens? Now you swear that you are! If you were a man who knew what truth is you might have a chance. But now—no! You are a monster of iniquity. I don't believe you!" She left the note in plain sight where she always found his letters in her desk. The next morning the note was gone. And so was Andy. She did not see him for three days.

It came about that a dance was to be held at Beacon during the late summer. The cowboys let Jane know that it was something she could not very well afford to miss. She had not attended either of the cowboy dances which had been given since her arrival. This next one, however, appeared to be an annual affair, at which all the ranching fraternity for miles around would be attending. Jane, as a matter of fact, was wild to go. However, she felt that she could not accept the escort of any one of her cowboy admirers without alienating the others. And she began to have visions of this wonderful dance fading away without a chance of her attending, when Springer accosted her one day.

"Who's the lucky cowboy to take you to our dance?" he asked.

"He seems to be as mysterious and doubtful as Mr. Frank Owens," replied Jane.

"Oh, you still remember him," said the rancher, his keen dark eyes quizzically on her.

"Indeed I do," sighed Jane.

"Too bad! He was a villain. . . . But you don't mean you haven't been asked to go?"

"They've all asked me. That's the trouble."

"I see. But you mustn't miss it. It'd be pleasant for you to meet some of the ranchers and their wives. Suppose you go with me?"

"Oh, Mr. Springer, I—I'd be delighted," replied Jane.

"Thank you. Then it's settled. I must be in town all that day on cattle business—next Friday. I'll ask the Hartwells to stop here for you, an' drive you in."

He seemed gravely, kindly interested as always, yet there was something in his eyes that interfered with the regular beating of Jane's heart. She could not forget what the cowboys had told her, even if she dared not believe it.

Jane spent much of her remaining leisure hours on a gown to wear at the coming dance, which promised so much. And because of the labor, she saw little of the cowboys. Tex was highly offended with her and would not deign to notice her anyhow. She wondered what would happen at the dance. She was a little fearful, too, because she had already learned of what fire and brimstone these cowboys were made. So dreaming and conjecturing, now amused and again gravely pensive, Jane awaited the eventful night.

The Hartwells turned out to be nice people whose little girl was one of Jane's pupils. Their evident delight in the Missouri girl's appearance gave the adventure one more thrill of anticipation for her. She had been afraid to trust her own judgment as to how she looked. On the drive townward, through the crisp early-fall gloaming, while listening to the chatter of the children and the talk of the elder Hartwells, she could not help wondering what Springer would think of her in the new gown.

They arrived late, according to her escorts. The drive to town was sixteen miles, but it had seemed short to Jane. "Reckon it's just as well for you an' the children," said Mrs. Hartwell to Jane. "These dances last from seven to seven."

"No!" exclaimed Jane.

"They sure do."

"Well, you know I am a tenderfoot from Missouri. But that's not going to keep me from having a wonderful time."

"You will, honey, unless the cowboys wind up in a fight over you, which is quite likely. But at least there won't be any shootin'. My husband an' Springer are both on the committee an' they won't admit any gun-totin' cowpuncher."

In Mrs. Hartwell's remark Jane had concrete evidence of something she had begun to suspect. These careless, love-making cowboys might be dangerous. The thought thrilled while it repelled her.

Jane's first sight of that dance hall astonished her. It

was a big barnlike room, crudely raftered and sided, decorated with colored bunting which took away some of the bareness. The oil lamps were not bright, but there were plenty of them hung in brackets around the room. The volume of sound amazed her. Music and the trample of boots, gay laughter, the deep voices of men, and the high-pitched voices of the children—all seemed to merge into a loud, confused uproar. A swaying, wheeling horde of dancers circled past her. No more time, just then, was accorded her to view the spectacle, for Springer suddenly confronted her. He seemed different somehow. Perhaps it was because of the absence of his rancher's corduroys and boots. If Jane needed assurance of what she had dreamed and hoped for she had it now in his frank admiration.

"Sure it's something pretty fine for old Bill Springer to have the prettiest girl here," he said.

"Thank you—but, Mr. Springer—I can easily see that you were a cowboy before you became a rancher," she replied archly.

"Sure I was. And that you will be dead sure to find out," he laughed. "Of course I could never compete with—say—Frank Owens. But let's dance. I shall have little enough of you in this outfit."

So he swung her into the circle of dancers. Jane found him easy to dance with, though he was far from expert. It was a jostling mob, and she soon acquired a conviction that if her gown did outlast the entire dance her feet never would. Springer took his dancing seriously and had little to say. She felt strange and uncertain with him. Presently she became aware of the cessation of hum and movement. The music had stopped.

"That sure was the best dance I ever had," said Springer, with a glow of excitement on his dark face. "An' now I must lose you to this outfit just coming."

Manifestly he meant his cowboys, Tex, Nevada,

Panhandle, and Andy, who were presenting themselves four abreast, shiny of hair and face.

"Good luck," he whispered. "If you get into a jam, let me know."

What he meant quickly dawned upon Jane. Right then it began. She saw there was absolutely no use in trying to avoid or refuse these young men. The wisest and safest course was to surrender, which she did.

"Boys, don't all talk at once. I can dance with only one of you at a time. So I'll take you in alphabetical order. I'm a poor old schoolmarm from Missouri, you know. It'll be Andy, Nevada, Panhandle, and Tex."

Despite their protests she held rigidly to this rule. Each one of the cowboys took shameless advantage of his opportunity. Outrageously as they all hugged her, Tex was the worst offender. She tried to stop dancing, but he carried her along as if she had been a child. He was rapt, and yet there seemed a devil in him.

"Tex—how dare—you!" she panted, when at last the dance ended.

"Wal, I reckon I'd about dare anythin' fer you, Jane," he replied, towering over her.

"You ought to be—ashamed," she went on. "I'll not dance with you again."

"Aw, now," he pleaded.

"I won't, Tex, so there. You're no gentleman."

"Ahuh!" he retorted drawing himself up stiffly. "All right, I'll go out an' get drunk, an' when I come back I'll clean out this heah hall so quick that you'll get dizzy watchin'."

"Tex! Don't go," she called hurriedly, as he started to stride away. "I'll take that back. I will give you another dance—if you promise to—to behave."

With this hasty promise she got rid of him, and was carried off by Mrs. Hartwell to be introduced to the various ranchers and their wives, and to all the girls and their escorts. She found herself a center of admiring eyes. She promised more dances than she could ever hope to remember or keep.

Her next partner was a tall handsome cowboy named Jones. She did not know quite what to make of him. But he was an unusually good dancer, and he did not hold her in such a manner that she had difficulty in breathing. He talked all the time. He was witty and engaging, and he had a most subtly flattering tongue. Jane could not fail to grasp that he might even be more outrageous than Tex, but at least he did not make love to her with physical violence. She enjoyed that dance and admitted to herself that the singular forceful charm about this Mr. Jones was appealing. If he was a little too bold of glance and somehow too primitively self-assured and debonair she passed it by in the excitement and joy of the hour, and in the conviction that she was now a long way from Missouri. Jones demanded, rather than begged for, another dance, and though she laughingly explained her predicament in regard to partners he said he would come after her anyhow.

Then followed several dances with new partners, and Jane became more than ever the center of attraction. It all went to the schoolteacher's head like wine. She was having a perfectly wonderful time. Jones claimed her again, in fact whirled her away from the man to whom she was talking and out on the floor. Twice again before the supper hour at midnight she found herself dancing with Jones. How he managed it she did not know. He just took her, carrying her off by storm. She did not awaken to this unpardonable conduct of hers until she suddenly recalled that a little before she had promised Tex his second dance, and then she had given it to Jones, or at least had danced it with him. But, after all, what could she do when he had walked right off with her? It was a glimpse of Tex's face, as she was being whirled past in Jones's arms, that filled Jane with sudden remorse.

Then came the supper hour. It was a gala occasion, for which evidently the children had heroically kept awake. Jane enjoyed the children immensely. She sat with the numerous Hartwells, all of whom were most pleasantly attentive to her. Jane wondered why Mr. Springer did not put in an appearance, but considered his absence due to numerous duties on the dance committee!

When the supper hour ended and the people were stirring about the hall again, and the musicians were tuning up, Jane caught sight of Andy. He looked rather pale and almost sick. Jane tried to catch his eye, but failing that she went to him.

"Andy, please find Tex for me. I owe him a dance, and I'll give him the very first, unless Mr. Springer comes for it."

Andy regarded her with an aloofness totally new to her.

"Wal, I'll tell him. But I reckon Tex ain't presentable jist now. An' all of us boys are through dancin' fer tonight."

"What's happened?" asked Jane, swift to divine trouble.

"There's been a little fight."

"Oh, no!" cried Jane. "Who? Why?—Andy, please tell me."

"Wal, when you cut Tex's dance for Beady Jones, you shore put our outfit in bad," replied Andy coldly. "At thet there wouldn't have been anythin' come of it here if Beady Jones hadn't got to shootin' off his chin. Tex slapped his face an' thet shore started a fight. Beady licked Tex, too, I'm sorry to say. He's a pretty bad hombre, Beady is, an' he's bigger 'n Tex. Wal, we had a hell of a time keepin' Nevada out of it. Thet would have been a wuss fight. I'd like to have seen it. But we kept them apart till Springer come out. An' what the boss said to that outfit was sure aplenty. Beady Jones kept talkin' back, nasty-like—you know he was once foreman for us—till Springer got good an' mad. An' he said: 'Jones, I fired you once because you was a little too slick for our outfit, an' I'll tell you this, if it come to a pinch I'll give you the damnedest thrashin' any smart-aleck cowboy ever got.' . . . Judas, the boss was riled. It sort of surprised me, an' tickled me pink. You can bet thet shut Beady Jones's loud mouth mighty quick!''

After his rather lengthy speech, Andy left her unceremoniously standing there alone. She was not alone long, but it was long enough for her to feel a rush of bitter dissatisfaction with herself.

Jane looked for Springer, hoping yet fearing he would come to her. But he did not. She had another uninterrupted dizzy round of dancing until her strength completely failed. By four o'clock she was scarcely able to walk. Her pretty dress was torn and mussed; her white stockings were no longer white; her slippers were worn ragged. And her feet were dead. She dragged herself to a chair where she sat with Mrs. Hartwell, looking on, and trying to keep awake. The wonderful dance, that had begun so promisingly, had ended sadly for her.

At length the exodus began, though Jane did not see many of the dancers leaving. She went out with the Hartwells, to be received by Springer, who had evidently made arrangements for their leaving. He seemed decidedly cool to the remorseful Jane.

All during the long ride out to the ranch he never addressed her or looked toward her. Daylight came, appearing cold and gray to Jane. She felt as if she wanted to cry.

Springer's sister, and the matronly housekeeper

were waiting for them, with a cheery welcome, and an invitation to a hot breakfast.

Presently Jane found herself momentarily alone with the taciturn rancher.

"Miss Stacey," he said, in a voice she had never heard, "your crude flirting with Beady Jones made trouble for the Springer outfit last night."

"Mr. Springer!" she exclaimed, her head going up.

"Excuse me," he returned, in a cutting, dry tone that recalled Tex. After all, this Westerner was still a cowboy, just exactly like those who rode for him, only a little older, and therefore more reserved and careful of his speech. "If it wasn't that—then you sure appeared to be pretty much taken with Mr. Beady Jones."

"If that was anybody's business it might have appeared so," she retorted, tingling all over with some feeling which she could not control.

"Sure. But are you denying it?" he asked soberly, eyeing her with a grave frown and obvious disapproval. It was this more than his question that roused hot anger and contrariness in Jane.

"I admired Mr. Jones very much," she replied haughtily. "He was a splendid dancer. He did not maul me like a bear. I really had a chance to breathe during my dances with him. Then too he could talk. He was a gentleman."

Springer bowed with dignity. His dark face paled. It dawned upon Jane that the situation had become serious for everyone concerned. She began to repent of her hasty pride.

"Thanks," he said. "Please excuse my impertinence. I see you have found your Mr. Frank Owens in this cowboy Jones, and it sure is not my place to say any more."

"But—but—Mr. Springer—" faltered Jane, quite

unstrung by the rancher's amazing speech. However, he merely bowed again and left her. Jane felt too miserable and weary for anything but rest and a good cry. She went to her room, and flinging off her hateful finery she crawled into bed, and buried her head in her pillow.

About mid-afternoon Jane awakened, greatly refreshed and relieved, and strangely repentant. She dressed carefully and went out, not quite sure of or satisfied with herself. She walked up and down the long porch of the ranch house, gazing out over the purple range, and up to the black belt of forest up the mountains. How beautiful this Arizona! She loved it. Could she ever leave it? She hoped that the time would never come that she would have to face such a necessity. She invaded the kitchen, where the good-natured housekeeper, who had become fond of her, gave her some wild-turkey sandwiches and cookies and sweet rich milk. While Jane appeased her hunger the woman gossiped about the cowboys and Springer, and the information she imparted renewed Jane's concern over the last night's affair.

From the kitchen Jane went out into the courtyard, and naturally, as always, gravitated toward the corrals and barns. Springer appeared, in company with a rancher Jane did not know. She expected Springer to stop her for a few pleasant words as was his wont. This time, however, he merely touched his sombrero and passed on. Jane felt the incident almost as a slight. And it hurt.

As she went on down the land she became very thoughtful. A cloud suddenly had appeared above the horizon of her happy life there at the Springer ranch. It did not seem to her that what she had done deserved the change in everyone's attitude. The lane opened out into a wide square, around which were the gates to the corrals, the entrances to several barns, the forge, granaries, and the commodious bunkhouse of the cowboys.

Jane's sharp eyes caught sight of the boys before they saw her. But when she looked up again every broad back was turned. They allowed her to pass without any apparent knowledge of her existence. This obvious snub was unprecedented. It offended her bitterly. She knew that she was being unreasonable, but could not or would not help it. She strolled on down to the pasture gate, and watched the colts and calves. Upon her return she passed even closer to the cowboys. But again they apparently did not see her. Jane added resentment to her wounded vanity and pride. Yet even then a still small voice tormented and accused her. She went back to her room, meaning to read or sew, or prepare school work. But instead she sat down in a chair and burst into tears.

Springer did not put in an appearance at the dinner table; and that was the last straw for Jane. She realized that she had made a mess of her wonderful opportunity here. But those stupid fiery cowboys! This sensitive Westerner! How could she be expected to know how to take them? The worst of it was that she was genuinely fond of the cowboys. And as for the rancher, her mind seemed to be a little vague and not too sure about him, although she told herself that she hated him.

Next day was Sunday. Heretofore every Sunday had been a full day for Jane. This one, however, bade fair to be an empty one. Company came as usual, neighbors from nearby ranches. The cowboys were off duty and other cowboys came over to visit them.

Jane's attention was attracted by sight of a superb horseman riding up the lane to the ranch house. He seemed familiar, somehow, but she could not place him. What a picture he made as he dismounted, slick and shiny, booted and spurred, to doff his huge sombrero! Jane heard him ask for Miss Stacey. Then she recognized him. Beady Jones! She was at once horrified, and yet attracted to this cowboy. She remembered now he had asked if he might call Sunday and she had certainly not refused to see him. But for him to come here after the fight with Tex and the bitter scene with Springer! It seemed almost an unparalleled affront. What manner of man was this cowboy Jones? He certainly did not lack courage. But more to the point—what idea had he of her? Jane rose to the occasion. She had let herself in for this, and she would see it through, come what might. Looming disaster stimulated her. She would show these indifferent deceitful, fire-spirited, incomprehensible cowboys! She would let Springer see that she indeed had taken Beady Jones for Mr. Frank Owens.

With this thought in mind, Jane made her way down the porch to greet her cowboy visitor. She made herself charming and gracious, and carried off the embarrassing situation—for Springer was present— just as if it were the most natural thing in the world. And she led Jones to one of the rustic benches farther down the porch.

Jane meant to gauge him speedily, if that were possible. While she made conversation she brought to bear all that she possessed in the way of intuition and discernment. The situation here was easy for her.

Naturally Jones resembled the cowboys she knew. The same range and life had developed him. But she could see that he lacked certain things which she liked so much in Tex and Nevada. He was a superb animal. She had reluctantly to admire his cool boldness in a situation certainly not altogether easy for him. But then he must have reasoned, of course, that she would be his protection. She did not fail to note that he carried a gun inside his embroidered vest.

Obvious, indeed, was it in all his actions that young Jones felt he had made a conquest. He was the most forceful and bold person Jane had ever met, quite incapable of appreciating her as a lady. It was not long before he was waxing ardent. Jane had become accustomed to the sentimental talk of cowboys, but this fellow was neither amusing nor interesting. He was dangerous. When she pulled her hand, by main force, free from his, and said she was not accustomed to allow men such privileges, he grinned at her like the handsome devil he was.

"Sure, sweetheart, you have missed a heap of fun," he said. "An' I reckon I'll have to break you in."

Jane could not really feel insulted at this brazen, conceited fool, but she certainly could feel enraged with herself. Her instant impulse was to excuse herself and abruptly leave him. But Springer was close by. She had caught his dark, speculative, covert glances. And the cowboys were at the other end of the long porch. Jane feared another fight. She had brought this situation upon herself, and she must stick it out. The ensuing hour was an increasing torment. At last it seemed to her that she could not bear the false situation any longer. And when Jones again importuned her to meet him out on horseback some time, she stooped to deception to end the interview. She really did not concentrate her attention on his plan or really take stock of what she was agreeing to do, but she got rid of him with ease and dignity in the presence of Springer and the others. After that she did not have the courage to stay out there and face them. How bitterly she had disappointed them all! Jane stole off to the darkness and loneliness of her room. There, however, she was not above peeping out from behind her window blind at the cowboys. They had grown immeasurably in her estimation. Alas! But now, no doubt, they were through with the little tenderfoot schoolmarm from Missouri.

3

THE SCHOOL TEACHING WENT ON JUST THE SAME, and the cowboys thawed out perceptibly, and Springer returned somewhat to his friendly manner, but Jane missed something from her work and in them, and her heart was sad the way everything was changed. Would it ever be the same again? What had happened? She had only been an emotional little tenderfoot unused to Western ways. After all, she had not failed, at least in gratitude and affection, though now it seemed they would never know.

There came a day, when Jane rode off alone toward the hills. She forgot the risk and all of the admonitions of the cowboys. She wanted to be alone to think. She was unhappy. Her work, the children, the friends she had made, even the horse she loved, were no longer all-sufficient. Something had come over her. She tried to persuade herself that she was homesick or just plain morbid. But she was not honest with herself and she knew it.

It was late fall, but the sun was warm that afternoon, and it was the season when little wind prevailed. Before her lay the valley range, a green-gray expanse dotted with cattle. Beyond it the cedared foothills rose, and above them loomed the dark beckoning mountains. Her horse was fast and liked to run with her. She loved him and the open range, with the rushing air in her face, and all that clear, lonely, vast, and silent world before her. Never could she return to live in the crowded cities again, with their horde of complaining people. She had found health and life—and something else that stirred in her heart and stung her cheek.

She rode fast until her horse was hot and she was out of breath. Then she slowed down. The foothills seemed so close now. But they were not really close. Still she could smell the fragrant dry cedar aroma on the air.

Then for the first time she looked back toward the ranch. It was a long way off—ten miles—a mere green spot in the gray. Suddenly she caught sight of a horseman coming. As usual some one of the cowboys had observed her, let her think she had slipped away, and was now following her. Today it angered Jane. She wanted to be alone. She could take care of herself. And as was unusual with her, she used her quirt on the horse. He broke into a gallop. She did not look back again for a long time. When she did it was to discover that the horseman had not only gained, but was now quite close to her. Jane looked intently, but she could not recognize the rider. Once she imagined it was Tex and again Andy. It did not make any difference which one of the cowboys it was. She was angry, and if he caught up with her he would be sorry.

Jane rode the longest and fastest race she had ever ridden. She reached the low foothills, and without heeding the fact that she might speedily become lost, she entered the cedars and began to climb. She ascended a hill, went down the slope, up a ravine, only to climb again. At times her horse had to walk and then she would hear her pursuer breaking through the cedars. He had to trail her by her horse's tracks, and so she was able to keep well in the lead. It was not long before she realized that she was lost, but she did not care. She rode up and down and around for an hour, until she was thoroughly tired out, and then upon the top of a steep hill she reined in her horse and waited to give her pursuer a piece of her mind.

What was her amazement when she heard a thud of hoofs and crackling of branches in the opposite direction from which she was expecting her pursuer, and saw a rider emerge from the cedars and trot his horse toward her. Jane needed only a second glance to recognize Beady Jones. Surely she had met him by chance. Suddenly she knew that he was not the pursuer she had been so angrily aware of. Jones's horse was white. That checked her mounting anger.

Jones rode straight at her, and as he came close Jane saw his bold tanned face and gleaming eyes. Instantly she realized that she had been mad to ride so far into the wild country, to expose herself to something from which the cowboys on the ranch had always tried to save her.

"Howdy, sweetheart," sang out Jones, in his cool, devil-may-care way. "Reckon it took you a long time to make up your mind to meet me as you promised."

"I didn't ride out to meet you, Mr. Jones," replied Jane spiritedly. "I know I agreed to something or other, but even then I didn't mean it."

"Yes, I had a hunch you was jist playin' with me," he returned darkly, riding his white mount right up against her horse.

He reached out a long gloved hand and grasped her arm.

"What do you mean, sir?" demanded Jane, trying to wrench her arm free.

"Shore I mean a lot," he said grimly. "You stood for the love-makin' of that Springer outfit. Now you're goin' to get a taste of somethin' not quite so easy."

"Let go of me—you—you ruffian!" cried Jane, struggling fiercely. She was both furious and terrified. But she seemed to be a child in the grasp of a giant.

"Hell! Your fightin' will only make it more interestin'. Come here, you sassy little cat."

And he lifted her out of her saddle over onto his horse in front of him. Jane's mount, that had been frightened and plunging, ran away into the cedars. Then Jones proceeded to embrace Jane. She managed to keep her mouth from contact with his, but he kissed her face and neck, kisses that seemed to fill her with shame and disgust.

"Jane, I'm ridin' out of this country fer good," he said. "An' I've jist been waitin' fer this chance. You bet you'll remember Beady Jones."

Jane realized that Jones would stop at nothing. Frantically she fought to get away from him, and to pitch herself to the ground. She screamed. She beat and tore at him. She scratched his face till the blood flowed. And as her struggles increased with her fright, she gradually slipped down between him and the pommel of his saddle, with head hanging down on one side and her feet on the other. This position was awkward and painful, but infinitely preferable to being crushed in his arms. He was riding off with her as if she had been a half-empty sack. Suddenly Jane's hands, while trying to hold on to something to lessen the severe jolting her position was giving her, came in contact with Jones's gun. Dare she draw it and shoot him? Then all at once her ears filled with the approaching gallop of another horse. Inverted as she was, she was able to see and recognize Springer riding directly at Jones and yelling hoarsely.

Next she felt Jones's hard jerk at his gun. But Jane had hold of it, and suddenly her little hands had the strength of steel. The fierce energy with which Jones was wrestling to draw his gun threw Jane from the saddle. And when she dropped clear of the horse the gun came with her.

"Hands up, Beady!" she heard Springer call out, as she lay momentarily face down in the dust. Then she struggled to her knees, and crawled to get away from the danger of the horses' hoofs. She still clung to the heavy gun. And when breathless and almost collapsing she fell back on the ground, she saw Jones with his hands above his head and Springer on foot with leveled gun.

"Sit tight, cowboy," ordered the rancher, in a hard tone. "It'll take damn little to make me bore you."

Then while still covering Jones, evidently ready for any sudden move, Springer spoke again.

"Jane, did you come out to meet this cowboy?" he asked.

"Oh, no! How can you ask that?" cried Jane, almost sobbing.

"She's a liar, boss," spoke up Jones coolly. "She let me make love to her. An' she agreed to ride out an' meet me. Wal, it shore took her a spell, an' when she did come she was shy on the love-makin'. I was packin' her off to scare some sense into her when you rode in."

"Beady, I know your way with women. You can save your breath, for I've a hunch you're going to need it."

"Mr. Springer," faltered Jane, getting to her knees. "I—I was foolishly attracted to this cowboy—at first. Then—that Sunday after the dance when he called on me at the ranch—I saw through him then. I heartily despised him. To get rid of him I did say I'd meet him. But I never meant to. Then I forgot all about it. Today I rode alone for the first time. I saw someone following me and thought it must be Tex or one of the boys. Finally I waited, and presently Jones rode up to me. . . . And Mr. Springer, he—he grabbed me off my horse—and handled me most brutally—shamefully. I

217

fought him with all my might, but what could I do?"

Springer's face changed markedly during Jane's long explanation. Then he threw his gun on the ground in front of Jane.

"Jones, I'm going to beat you within an inch of your life," he said grimly; and leaping at the cowboy he jerked him out of the saddle and sent him sprawling on the ground. Next Springer threw aside his sombrero, his vest, his spurs. But he kept on his gloves. The cowboy rose to one knee, and he measured the distance between him and Springer, and then the gun that lay on the ground. Suddenly he sprang toward it. But Springer intercepted him with a powerful kick that tripped Jones and laid him flat.

"Jones, you're sure about as lowdown as they come," he said, in a tone of disgust. "I've got to be satisfied with beating you when I ought to kill you."

"Ahuh! Wal, boss, it ain't any safe bet thet you can do either," returned Jones sullenly, as he got up.

As they rushed together Jane had wit enough to pick up the gun, and then with it and Jones's, to get back to a safe distance. She wanted to run away out of sight. But she could not keep her fascinated gaze from the combatants. Even in her distraught condition she could see that the cowboy, young and active and strong as he was, could not hold his own with Springer. They fought over all the open space, and crashed into the cedars and out again. The time came when Jones was on the ground about as much as he was erect. Bloody, dishevelled, beaten, he kept on trying to stem the onslaught of blows.

Suddenly he broke off a dead branch of cedar, and brandishing it rushed at the rancher. Jane uttered a cry, closed her eyes, and sank to the ground. She heard fierce muttered imprecations and savage blows. When at length she opened her eyes again, fearing something dreadful, she saw Springer erect, wiping his face with the back of one hand, and Jones lying on the ground.

Then Jane saw him go to his horse, untie a canteen from the saddle, remove his bloody gloves, and wash his face with a wet scarf. Next he poured some water on Jones's face.

"Come on, Jane," he called. "Reckon it's all over."

He tied the bridle of Jones's horse to a cedar, and leading his own animal turned to meet Jane.

"I want to compliment you on getting that cowboy's gun," he said warmly. "But for that there'd sure have been something bad. I'd have had to kill him, Jane. . . . Here, give me the guns. . . . You poor little tenderfoot from Missouri. No, not tenderfoot any longer. You became a Westerner today."

His face was bruised and cut, his clothes dirty and bloody, but he did not appear the worse for such a desperate fight. Jane found her legs scarcely able to support her, and she had apparently lost her voice.

"Let me put you on my saddle till we find your horse," he said, and lifted her lightly as a feather to a seat crosswise in the saddle. Then he walked with a hand on the bridle.

Jane saw him examining the ground, evidently searching for horse tracks. "Ha! here we are." And he led off in another direction through the cedars. Soon Jane saw her horse, calmly nibbling at the bleached grass. In a few moments she was back in her own saddle, beginning to recover somewhat from her terrifying experience. But she seemed to realize that as fast as she recovered from one set of emotions she was going to be plunged into another. "There's a good cold spring down here in the rocks," remarked Springer. "I think you need a drink, and so do I."

They rode down the sunny cedar slopes into a shady

ravine skirted by pines, and up to some mossy cliffs from which a spring gushed forth.

Jane was now in the throes of several thrilling, bewildering, conflicting hopes and fears. Why had Springer followed her? Why had he not sent one of the cowboys? Why did she feel so afraid and foolish? He had always been courteous and kind and thoughtful; at least until she had offended him so egregiously. And here he was now! He had fought for her. Would she ever forget? Her heart began to pound. And when he dismounted to help her off her horse she knew it was to see a scarlet and telltale face.

"Mr. Springer, I—I thought you were Tex—or somebody," she said.

He laughed as he took off his sombrero. His face was warm, and the cuts were still bleeding a little.

"You sure can ride," he replied. "And that's a good little pony."

He loosened the cinches on the horses. Jane managed to hide some of her confusion.

"Won't you walk around a little?" he asked. "It'll rest you. We are fifteen miles from home."

"So far?"

Then presently he helped her to her feet and stood beside her with a hand on her horse. He looked frankly into her face. The keen eyes were softer than usual. He looked so fine and strong and splendid that she found herself breathing with difficulty. She was afraid of her betraying eyes and looked away.

"When the boys found that you were gone they all saddled up to find you," he said. "But I asked them if they didn't think the boss ought to have one chance. So they let me come."

Right about then something completely unforeseen happened to Jane's heart. She was overwhelmed by a strange happiness that she knew she ought to hide, but could not. She could not speak. The silence grew. She felt Springer there, but she could not look at him.

"Do you like it out here in the West?" he asked presently.

"Oh, I love it! I'll never want to leave it," she replied impulsively.

"I reckon I'm glad to hear you say that."

Then there fell another silence. He pressed closer to her and seemed now to be leaning against the horse. She wondered if he heard the thunderous knocking of her heart against her side.

"Will you be my wife an' stay here always?" he asked simply. "I'm in love with you. I've been lonely since my mother died. . . . You'll sure have to marry some one of us. Because, as Tex says, if you don't, ranching can't go on much longer. These boys don't seem to get anywhere with you. Have I any chance— Jane?"

He possessed himself of her gloved hand and gave her a gentle tug. Jane knew that it was gentle because she scarcely felt it. Yet it had irresistible power. She was swayed by that gentle pull. She moved into his arms.

A little later he smiled at her and said, "Jane, they call me Bill for short. Same as they call me Boss. But my two front names are Frank Owens."

"Oh!" cried Jane startled. "Then you—you—"

"Yes, I'm the guilty one," he replied happily. "It happened this way. My bedroom, you know, is next to my office. I often heard the boys pounding the typewriter. I had a hunch they were up to some trick. So I spied upon them—heard about Frank Owens and the letters to the little schoolmarm. At Beacon I got the postmistress to give me your address. And, of course, I intercepted some of your letters. It sure has turned out great."

"I—I don't know about you or those terrible cowboys," replied Jane dubiously. "How did *they* happen on the name Frank Owens?"

"That's sure a stumper. I reckon they put a job up on me."

"Frank—tell me—did *you* write the—the love letters?" she asked appealingly. "There were two kinds of letters. That's what I could never understand."

"Jane, I reckon I did," he confessed. "Something about your little notes made me fall in love with you clear back there in Missouri. Does that make it all right?"

"Yes, Frank, I reckon it does—now," she returned.

"Let's ride back home and tell the boys," said Springer gayly. "The joke's sure on them. I've corralled the little 'under-forty schoolmarm from Missouri.'"

D

MAX BRAND

THE MASTER OF TWO-FISTED WESTERN ADVENTURE

___The Blue Jay 54087/$2.50

___Destry Rides Again 83660/$2.50

___Fightin' Fool 41579/$2.25

___The Longhorn Feud
41559/$2.50

___Rawhide Justice 41589/$2.50

___Singing Guns 41571/$2.25

___The Streak 41576/$2.25